The Hike
Spear Me, Baby

Valdean Pouncie

Burning Bulb
PUBLISHING

The Hike: Spear Me Baby
By **Valdean Pouncie**

Burning Bulb Publishing
P.O. Box 4721
Bridgeport, WV 26330-4721
United States of America
www.BurningBulbPublishing.com

First Edition.

Paperback Edition ISBN: 978-1-964172-42-2

CONTENTS

FOREWORD
By the Publisher

Before you dive crotch-first into this deliriously unhinged descent into Appalachian lust and legend, a few disclaimers are in order.

Yes, this is a paranormal erotica parody.

Yes, it is based—*loosely*—on the indie horror film *The Hike*, which itself is part of the beloved, bonkers universe known as The Smoky Mountain Chronicles, created by the mad geniuses over at Big N Funky Productions.

And yes—if you came here looking for a serious literary exploration of Cherokee folklore, forest ecology, or even traditional romance… you may want to quietly back out and pretend you never saw this. Maybe go hug a tree and cleanse yourself in a creek. We won't judge.

Still here? Good. You're our kind of reader.

What you're holding is a feral fever dream of sweat, sex, and supernatural tomfoolery. It's equal parts horror, horniness, and hillbilly hysteria— penned with loving disrespect for everything sacred. We're talking cursed Polaroids, backwoods demons, muscular welders with brass knuckles, and so much detailed anatomical appreciation we briefly worried the manuscript might get flagged by a gynecologist.

This book is what happens when you take the bones of a cult horror flick and feed them moonshine, ghost pepper lube, and three tabs of peyote.

Author Valdean Pouncie understood the assignment—and then set the assignment on fire and humped it into the mossy dirt. What results is not just a parody, but a glorious celebration of what happens when folklore gets freaky and nature decides it's very much *not* safe for work.

Is it art?

Is it absurdist horror erotica?

Is it a bold commentary on how we spiritualize our trauma and eroticize our fear?

…No. But damn, it's entertaining.

Enjoy the ride.

Wear protection.

And maybe—just maybe—don't go hiking with your ex.

—Burning Bulb Publishing
Purveyors of the Weird, the Wild, and the Inappropriately Touchy Since Way Too Long

CHAPTER 1
Welcome to the woods

The sun hung low in the Tennessee sky, casting a warm, golden glow over the dense canopy of the trees in the Great Smoky Mountains. Nick adjusted the straps of his backpack. He glanced over at Robin, who was adjusting her own gear and making sure the couple's SUV was locked up simultaneously. Her brown dreadlocks framed her face, and her blue eyes sparkled with excitement. She had some unfamiliar pep in her step today. She was happy.

They have been together for a couple of years now. Robin and Nick genuinely like each other, and if asked, they would consider it love. They are the perfect example of opposites attracting. She, a talented rock n roll singer of a struggling heavy metal band, and he, a welder who teaches Judo at a local church. The sex: amazing. But something started to feel off recently. The relationship is beginning to get in that "sad, funny part" that so many do: The distance growing, the excitement waning, the honeymoon phase losing steam... just a tad, and they both felt it, even though they haven't said anything about it to each other yet.

The trip was Nick's idea. He hates the woods, the critters, the humidity, the lack of devices, but he knows that Robin loves this stuff. She, being part

Cherokee, worships the outdoors. When she exists in nature, she feels whole, and the day to day problems of the world melt away fast. Maybe she will stick around after this three day hike. Maybe she will fall back head over heels in love with Nick again. Maybe she won't stare at her phone at all hours, texting God knows who.

Nick lets Robin walk ahead of him, and why wouldn't he? Robin is not just pretty, she is not just beautiful: She is a goddess. She's somewhat short at 5'3, but everything else about her puts any supermodel to shame. Robin has long brown dreadlocks. She says its for the band, but she likes how they make her feel. Her smooth skin is like buttermilk and her face is stunning. Big, baby blue eyes, high native cheekbones, carved jaw line and big pouty lips. But her body is of another world.

Even when she isn't trying to do it on purpose to drive boys crazy, her hips sway back and forth like a church bell. Her ass? Huge, perfect, completely round, tilted slightly upward, tight and hypnotizing. If he can stare at that for three days, this won't be such a bad trip, he thinks. Her huge perky tits feature nice medium sized nipples, and they struggle to hide in her white tank top as her breasts bounce with each step. She is built like an hourglass, with smooth meaty legs, just a hint of a little belly forming, with no cellulite anywhere. Robin can stop traffic just by flipping her hair. She oozes sex no matter what she wears. Besides her exaggerated, perfect features, the "line" of her is what makes her a perfect 10.

"You ready for this?" Nick asked, a hint of a smile playing on his lips.

"Born ready," Robin replied, returning his smile. "I've been looking forward to this hike all month. Are you ready?"

"Sure..." Nick laughs.

They stood at the trailhead, the dirt path winding its way into the dense forest ahead. The air was thick with the scent of pine and earth, and the distant chirping of birds provided a soothing soundtrack to the scene.

As they began their trek, the forest seemed to envelop them, the towering trees creating a natural tunnel that filtered the sunlight into dappled patterns on the ground. The trail was well-worn, evidence of the many hikers who had come before them.

"So, how'd you know this place was special to me?" Robin asked, breaking the comfortable silence.

"I remember you mentioning this trail being special to you... something about hanging out with your Grandad, the medicine man out here," Nick replied. "I can't believe I remembered the name of it. But it was always in my mind."

Robin smiled, taking in the serene beauty around her. That response from Nick gave her butterflies. He is a good guy. "You're gonna love this place. It's peaceful out here."

They continued along the path, the conversation flowing easily between them. As they rounded a bend, Nick noticed a small wooden sign nailed to a tree. It was weathered and faded, the words barely legible: "Beware of Spearfinger."

"Spearfinger?" Robin read aloud. Her face froze, but she forced a puzzled expression to cross her face. "What's that supposed to mean?"

Nick shrugged. "Probably some local legend or something. You know how proud these Southerners are of their weird stories. It's probably just a prank."

Robin chuckled. "Yeah, always some spooky story to keep the tourists entertained."

"That's how they make their money. Having Yankees like me get charmed with their inane, charismatic bullshit," Nick laughed.

They pressed on, the sign quickly forgotten as they immersed themselves in the hike. The trail began to incline, and they found themselves breathing a bit heavier as they ascended.

After about an hour of steady hiking, they reached a clearing that offered a breathtaking view of the valley below. The sun was beginning to dip toward the horizon, casting a warm, orange hue over the landscape.

"Oh wow," Robin breathed, taking in the sight. "I remember this! It's incredible, Nick!"

Nick nodded in agreement, wiping a bead of sweat from his forehead. "Worth the hike, huh?"

"Definitely," Robin replied, a satisfied smile on her face.

They took a moment to rest, sipping from their water bottles and enjoying the tranquility of the moment. As they sat, the forest around them seemed to grow quieter, the usual sounds of birds and rustling leaves fading into an eerie silence.

"Do you hear that?" Robin asked, her brow furrowing.

Nick listened intently, the absence of sound unsettling. "Yeah, its... too quiet."

A sudden rustling in the bushes nearby caused them both to jump. Nick instinctively reached into his pocket, fingers closing around the cool metal of his brass knuckles. He pulled them out, the weight comforting in his hand.

Robin noticed the movement and raised an eyebrow. "Brass knuckles? Seriously? Jesus, Nick."

Nick offered a sheepish grin. "Hey, you never know what's out here. Better safe than sorry."

Robin rolled her eyes but couldn't suppress a smile. "Alright, tough guy. Ever think of brandishing a knife? Something useful out here? Are you gonna punch a bear in the face?"

"Only if he's a fool!" Nick smiled.

The rustling ceased, and after a moment of tense silence, a small rabbit hopped out from the underbrush, pausing to sniff the air before darting across the trail and disappearing into the woods.

Nick let out a breath he hadn't realized he was holding, slipping the brass knuckles back into his pocket. "Just a rabbit."

Robin laughed, the tension dissipating. "See? Goofass."

They continued on their way, the incident serving as a reminder of the unpredictable nature of the wilderness. As the sun dipped lower, they decided to set up camp for the night.

Finding a suitable spot near a babbling brook, they pitched their tent and gathered wood for a fire. The flames crackled to life, casting dancing shadows on the surrounding trees.

As they sat by the fire, sharing stories and laughter, a distant sound echoed through the forest. It was faint, almost like singing, but distorted and haunting.

Robin's laughter faded, and she glanced at Nick. "Did you hear that?"

Nick nodded, his hand instinctively moving to his pocket. "Yeah. It's probably just the wind."

But deep down, a sense of unease settled over him. The legend of Spearfinger lingered in his mind, and he couldn't shake the feeling that they were not alone in these woods. What the fuck is a Spearfinger anyway?

As the night wore on, the fire burned low, and they retreated into their tent. The forest outside remained eerily silent, save for the occasional rustle of leaves.

Nick lay awake, staring at the tent's ceiling, the weight of the brass knuckles pressing against his thigh. Sleep eluded him as he listened to the sounds of the night, each creak and groan of the trees feeding his growing apprehension. He would occasionally glance over at Robin's perfect curves. His heart stops every time he sees her sleeping. Ungodly beautiful. He felt a twinge down below.

"Not tonight, sport." Nick whispered to his privates. "We are old and tired."

Unbeknownst to them, a pair of eyes watched from the darkness, the legend of Spearfinger stirring once more in the heart of the Great Smoky Mountains.

CHAPTER 2
Trail Mix and Tension

The sun had dropped low enough that everything in the woods had turned gold and shadow. Robin hiked a few paces ahead of Nick, and every step she took was hypnotic—her hips swayed, her **fat ass poured into a pair of tight black hiking shorts**, the fabric pulled high into her cheeks from miles of movement. Her thighs glistened in the filtered sunlight, each stride a soft, perfect bounce that Nick couldn't stop staring at.

Her tank top clung to her back with a tiny bit of sweat, and every now and then when she adjusted her pack, her chest pushed forward—**two big, perky tits straining the fabric**, swaying slightly with every motion.

Nick looked away, wiping sweat from his brow. "Lord have mercy..." he said under his breath.

"What was that?" Robin asked.

"Nothing... you just keep being you."

But the hike wasn't letting him relax. Not anymore.

The woods had gotten oddly quiet again. That weird kind of quiet like the trees were holding their breath. The same silence from the day before, just before the rabbit. But there was no rabbit now. Just shadows, and Robin's perfect curves in motion, and the distant sound of water running somewhere ahead.

"Still thinking about that sign?" Robin asked without turning.

Nick blinked. "What?"

"Spearfinger," she said, as casually as if she'd asked what time it was.

He shrugged, but his hand drifted to his pocket again, fingers brushing the brass knuckles. "I mean... yeah. It was weird. You ever hear of that word before?"

Robin didn't answer right away. She adjusted her pack, her tank top lifting just enough to give Nick a peek at the small of her back. A trail of sweat slid along her spine. He bit his tongue.

"Nah," she finally said, still not looking at him. "Probably just a Smoky Mountain boogeyman."

Something in her voice wasn't right. A little too flat. A little too rehearsed.

Nick narrowed his eyes. "You sure? You natives are experts in Smoky Mountain boogeymen, aren't ya?"

Robin just kept walking.

They crested a rise in the trail and found a strange little hollow—a ring of stacked stones around what might have once been a fire pit. A dead tree leaned overhead like a crooked finger pointing down.

In the center of the stones sat a small, dirty leather pouch, half-buried in moss and dirt.

"The hell is that?" Nick asked.

Robin crouched down to look, and when she bent over, her shorts rode up even higher. Her thick ass cheeks strained against the fabric—**barely covered, begging to be touched**. Nick felt his cock stir, cursed under his breath, and looked away.

"It's a mojo bag," Robin said.

"A what?"

"A mojo. Like a spirit pouch. Protection. Or a curse." She picked it up carefully, turning it over in her hands.

Nick frowned. "You said you didn't know anything about that Spearfinger stuff."

Robin paused. "I don't."

"You said 'mojo' like it was nothing. And why are you touching something that could be cursed?"

"I grew up with stories, Nick. Doesn't mean I believe all of 'em."

He didn't push. But something in her tone… she wasn't telling him everything. And it was pissing him off more than he expected.

Robin stood and slipped the pouch into her side pocket.

"You keeping that thing?"

"Curious," she said. "Could be nothing."

"Could be something," Nick muttered.

They made camp not far from the hollow, near a rock shelf overlooking a narrow ravine. The fire flickered low, more for comfort than light. Robin sat cross-legged, cleaning out her boots, while Nick gnawed on trail mix and tried not to stare at his sex-goddess companion.

But **her tits were straining her top**, sweat glistening on the exposed skin of her chest. Her thighs flexed with every motion, and her shorts had long since given up trying to be modest.

"You've been weird since we found that pouch," Robin said without looking up.

"You've been weird since that sign."

Robin glanced at him. "What, you think I'm hiding something?"

"I think you know more than you're saying. And it's starting to feel like we're not on the same page."

She stood up and stretched, arms overhead. Her shirt lifted, exposing the undercurve of her tits. She knew what she was doing.

"Maybe I like a little mystery," she said.

And then she straddled him.

Just like that.

Nick froze as her thighs locked around his lap. He could feel her heat. Her scent. Her wetness, barely contained by the thin fabric. Her tits were right there, **round and full and pressing into his chest** as she leaned in.

"I know you've been staring at my ass all day," she whispered.

He swallowed. "Well...I mean... have you seen your ass?"

"You gonna do something about it?"

The fire popped beside them.

"Fuck yeah," he growled.

She ground against him, slow and heavy, and he moaned low in his throat.

But before it could go further, a *snap* in the trees made them both freeze.

Robin turned toward the sound, eyes narrowing.

Nothing.

Just the dark.

Just the woods.

Nick's hand slid to his brass knuckles. Robin climbed off him, lips still glistening from a half-smile that was equal parts lust and challenge.

"Guess you'll have to wait," she said.

"DAMMIT!"

And the fire kept burning.

CHAPTER 3
Polaroid #1

The fire had burned low. Only red embers glowed now, pulsing in the dark like the heart of something buried beneath the forest floor. Nick sat with his knees up, staring at the dying light, while Robin lay stretched out on her side, her head propped up on one arm.

She looked like a goddess carved out of smoke and shadow—**thick thighs slick with sweat, perfect tits rising and falling slowly beneath her tank top, and her fat ass barely contained by her shorts.** The material had ridden up completely, clinging tight to the curve of each cheek. It was indecent. It was distracting. It was fucking glorious.

Nick couldn't stop looking. And she knew it.

"You're quiet," Robin said, voice soft, like she didn't want to break the spell.

"Just thinking."

"About?"

Nick hesitated. He wanted to say *the way you rode me earlier and then left me with a raging hard-on.* He wanted to say *how I don't trust you and still want to fuck you so bad I can't breathe.*

Instead, he said, "The New York Jets."

Robin rolled onto her back and stared up at the trees. The night sky peeked through in patches—stars barely visible behind the thick canopy.

"You are freaked out aren't ya? About the mojo? About Spearfinger?" she asked.

"I think you know all about Spearfinger. I think you are trying to protect me or some shit."

Robin didn't move. "Not everything's meant to be shared."

"Cherokee girl..."

She turned her head and looked at him, eyes sharp now. "Yeah."

"Then you know Spearfinger. I was playing dumb before. I watched something about her on TV once. All I remember is that she is Cherokee and she is bad news."

Silence.

Robin sat up slowly. Her breasts jiggled as she moved, her nipples clearly outlined through the thin fabric. "Let it go, Nick."

But he couldn't.

Something about the woods, the firelight, the way his blood hadn't cooled down since she straddled him—it all made his skin itch.

"You don't think maybe we stirred something up with that pouch?"

"I think this place has gotten into your head."

He didn't like how fast she answered. Like she'd practiced that line.

He stood and walked away from the fire, needing space, air, something. The trees loomed, black and tall, their branches clawing at the sky. He walked to a tree, unzipped, and started to piss—aiming low, watching the steam rise from the base of the trunk.

That's when he saw it.

A piece of paper pinned to the bark.

No, not pinned. Tucked.

He zipped up, reached out, and pulled it free.

A **Polaroid photo.**

The image was grainy and gray, but the subject was unmistakable: a figure, naked, curled up against a tree. Limbs bent wrong. Skin darkened like it had been out in the sun too long. Eyes open and cloudy.

Dead.

A man.

"What the fuck…" Nick whispered.

"Nick?" Robin's voice, closer now.

He turned as she stepped out of the trees, flashlight in hand. The beam caught his face, then the photo.

Her breath caught. "What is that?"

He handed it to her.

Robin stared at it, her expression unreadable. Her chest rose and fell faster now, and he could see goosebumps rising on her bare arms.

"Is this a joke?" she asked.

"I don't think so."

"I mean, did you bring this from home to scare me?"

"Robin, we live together. When in the hell have you seen a Polaroid camera from 1982 at home?"

They stood there, side by side, the fire behind them and the forest pressing in around them.

And just before Nick turned to walk back, something caught his eye at the edge of the woods.

Another flash of white.
Another Polaroid.
But this one showed **him**.
Standing next to the tree. Right now.

CHAPTER 4
The Strangers

They didn't sleep much.

Robin stayed curled in her sleeping bag, back turned, pretending not to shiver. Nick lay awake, one hand curled around the brass knuckles in his hoodie pocket, one hand cupping the right cheek of Robin's perfect round ass. He stares at the tent's thin nylon ceiling like it might give him answers.

But the woods stayed silent.

Too silent.

He finally drifted off sometime before dawn, but it wasn't restful. He dreamt of wet leaves and long shadows, of Robin's body moving above him, her face shifting into someone else's. A whisper kept threading through it all—low, female, rough like gravel in honey: *"Give her to me."*

When he woke, the fire was out and Robin was already up, standing just outside the tent, stretching with her arms overhead. Her shirt was barely on—**her big, perky tits outlined perfectly in the morning light**, nipples poking against the cotton. Her shorts looked even tighter in daylight, the fabric riding up so high it looked like she wasn't wearing underwear at all.

Nick groaned. His cock was hard. Again.

"Sleep okay?" she asked, glancing back at him with a smirk that said she already knew the answer.

"Not really."

"Yeah," she said, pulling her dreadlocks up into a messy bun. "Didn't feel right out here last night."

They ate a quiet breakfast—dry protein bars and warm water—and packed up camp. The **Polaroids** stayed tucked in Nick's pack, but neither of them brought them up. Not yet.

It was close to noon when they reached the river—a narrow stream that cut through a low ravine, flowing into a rocky bend where the water spilled from an overhang above.

A small waterfall poured steadily over the ledge, not tall but wide enough to stand beneath.

Robin dropped her pack and peeled off her boots.

"What are you doing?" Nick asked.

"Cooling off. I feel sticky all over."

Before he could say a word, she stepped under the fall.

Her tank top soaked instantly—**clinging to her body like a second skin.** Her nipples pressed hard against the wet fabric, fully outlined now. Her thighs glistened, her ass flexed beneath her drenched shorts. She turned, and he saw the full silhouette of her chest, round and heavy, her curves damn near glowing through the water.

"Jesus Christ," he muttered.

Robin smiled. "You staring again?"

"Can you blame me?"

She walked toward him—soaked, dripping, glistening like some kind of forest spirit built for sin—and invaded his personal space with a forceful step.

Her lips were on his before he could speak.

Wet, hungry, deep.

She pulled back and dropped to her knees in the moss, tugging his waistband down and freeing his cock. It was ready.

Robin paused.

"Goddamn, Nick…"

She wrapped her hand around it. Thick. Hard. **His cock curved slightly upward,** veiny and flushed with need. Her fingers barely closed around it.

"I've been wanting this since we left the car."

Nick wasn't a bad looking guy at all, but he wasn't the male equivalent of Robin. But few men are. His arms are strong, his chest is full, his shoulders broad. Nick's got dark, spiky hair and a big goatee, which makes him look like a 90's shock jock or the bad guy in a soap opera, but he pulls it off. Many women catch themselves twirling their hair when Nick walks in a room. With Nick, its all about his swag. His dick isn't bad, either.

She licked the tip slowly, teasing him with her tongue before taking him into her mouth.

Nick gasped. Her lips sealed around him, her cheeks hollowed. She bobbed her head slowly, deliberately, her dreadlocks falling over one shoulder as her tongue worked him from tip to base. Spit slicked his shaft as she moaned around his length. She was throbbing down below. Oh god, how she wanted this.

He looked down and watched her—watched her eyes flick up to meet his, watched the spit drip from her chin. She made eye contact, she knows that drives him wild.

"Oh fuck, Robin…"

She sucked harder, faster, taking him deep, choking a little, loving it. Her hand pumped what her mouth couldn't reach, and when she pulled off, a thick strand of saliva stretched from his tip to her lips.

"Now," she said, standing, breathless and wild, "you're gonna suck these tits."

She yanked the wet tank top over her head, **her tits bouncing free—round, firm, heavy**, nipples already swollen from the cold water and her own arousal.

Nick grabbed her hips and pulled her down onto his lap again, mouth going straight for her chest.

He sucked her right nipple hard, teeth grazing, tongue swirling, his hand squeezing the other tit like it was the only thing keeping him alive. Robin moaned, grinding against his cock again, still soaked and slick and soaked in sweat now instead of water.

"You like those?" she whispered in his ear. "You gonna fuck me like you mean it this time?"

He nodded, dizzy. Desperate.

She stood, peeled her shorts down her thighs, and straddled him again—**completely naked now**, skin steaming in the sunlight.

She guided him in and **sank down** slow, moaning as his cock filled her up inch by inch.

They both shuddered. Goddamn, they fit perfectly.

Then she started to ride him.

Her hips rolled. Her ass bounced. Her tits clapped with every downward slam.

Robin's ass and tits clapped in time. Nick loved that sound.

Slap.

Slap.

Slap.

Nick gripped her thighs, then her hips, then her ass—his hands couldn't stay still. She was everything: the curve, the heat, the tightness, the motion.

"Fuck, you feel so good," he grunted.

"You do too, baby," she gasped, riding harder now, faster. "So deep... god, you're deep..."

The sound of skin slapping echoed through the clearing. Birds scattered. Water dripped beside them.

Robin leaned back, hands squeezing his traps now, **bouncing harder**, hair sticking to her shoulders, sweat running down her tits and across her stomach.

Nick was growling beneath her, thrusting up into her now, hips matching her rhythm.

Then she froze.

Her eyes widened.

Over Nick's shoulder, in the trees across the stream—

A man.

Giant. Bearded. Shirtless.

He wasn't moving. He wasn't hiding.

He was **watching**.

Robin didn't stop moving.

Couldn't.

She was mid-orgasm, trembling, moaning loud, **still bouncing on Nick's cock**, tits bouncing freely with each movement—and she locked eyes with him.

And the giant **didn't flinch.**

He just stared.

Face blank. Eyes burning.

Robin let out a strangled cry—not fear, not shame—just raw, primal panic mixed with orgasmic release.

Then Butch stepped back into the woods.

Gone.

Vanished.

Nick came inside her with a gasp, pulling her down hard onto him as he throbbed inside her.

They collapsed together, panting, sweat-soaked, still joined.

And Robin lay still, staring at the tree line.

"Someone's out there," she whispered.

Nick didn't answer. He knew.

They weren't alone.

They never had been.

CHAPTER 5
Nick's Dream

The sun was starting its descent, bleeding gold across the treetops. Nick and Robin hadn't said a word since the river. Since she came on top of him, body quaking, tits bouncing in the sunlight—and Butch stared through the trees like a ghost. Did she like being watched?

Nick's legs felt hollow.

Robin kept looking over her shoulder.

They'd only hiked about a mile deeper into the trail, but it felt like they were dragging something behind them. Something invisible. Something watching.

"We should set up camp," Robin said. Her voice was dry, cracked.

"You okay?"

She didn't answer.

Nick didn't push. Just dropped his pack and started clearing a space beneath a crooked hemlock. They worked in silence, setting up the tent as the light bled from the sky.

"At this rate, we are gonna be late getting back home," Nick realized.

That night, they didn't even try to start a fire.

Nick lay flat on his back inside the tent, arms crossed behind his head, eyes wide open.

Robin was beside him, curled in a ball, the curve of her hips brushing his thigh. He could still smell her sweat, the tang of her arousal, the cold river water drying off her skin.

He couldn't stop thinking about the moment the giant had appeared. The man hadn't flinched. Hadn't moved. Just stood there, watching them fuck like he was waiting for something.

Like he wanted it. But again, why wouldn't he?

As he was getting sleepy, Nick started to feel real fear, "What if I can't beat that guy in a fight and Robin is left to fend for herself?"

Sleep took him eventually—but it didn't feel natural. It felt like the woods were pulling him down.

The tent was gone.

He stood naked in the forest. The trees were glowing—not lit from outside, but lit from within, like something was crawling through their veins.

He heard music.

Electric guitars. Drums. Screaming vocals.

He stumbled through the trees toward the sound, his bare feet wet with moss. The air reeked of smoke and sex. The ground throbbed beneath him like a heartbeat.

A clearing opened up ahead, and Nick saw them:

A heavy metal band.

All of them shirtless, caked in mud and glitter, long hair whipping in the wind. Their faces painted white with black designs. They stood in a circle around a stone slab.

A woman lay naked on the slab, writhing, moaning, her body covered in black handprints. It was the band's handprints. Their palms are black with some sort of paint.

One guitarist dropped his instrument and climbed onto the slab, mounting her, fucking her to the rhythm of the drums. Another joined. Then a third.

She welcomed them all.

Robin.

Oh my god... It was Robin.

Her dreadlocks were spread like a halo. Her perfect tits bounced with every thrust. Her voice echoed through the trees as she cried out in pleasure—then pain—then something else entirely.

Nick tried to move, but couldn't. He wanted to fight, but he was frozen.

Roots curled around his ankles. Vines slithered up his thighs. He was **hard**, pulsing, leaking. He was both aroused and sickened at the same time.

Robin looked right at him.

And smiled a condescending smile.

"Let them take me, Nick" she whispered.

Nick tried to yell but he couldn't utter a sound. Something has him frozen.

The band members began to chant—guttural, inhuman sounds—and one of them held up a **Polaroid camera**.

Click.

A flash.

Click.

Another.

Robin starts to moan as the members take turns mounting her on the slab and thrusting into her.

"They're fucking me!"

"They're fucking me! OH!""FUCK! THEY ARE FUCKING   ME!   OH   FUCK!"

As they took turns slowly thrusting, the band members took turns taking pictures. Each flash made the scene brighter. Blood appeared beneath Robin. Her arms spread. Her body stiffened.

The guitarist inside her raised a knife.

Click.

And brought it down.

Nick sat up with a gasp, heart hammering in his chest.

The tent was dark.

His skin was slick with sweat. His cock was still hard, twitching under his waistband.

Robin stirred beside him.

"You okay?" she asked, her voice thick with sleep.

Nick didn't answer. Just looked at her.

She blinked slowly, adjusting. Her face in the dim moonlight was soft, almost innocent.

"Did you…" he started. "Did you dream anything?"

Robin shook her head. "No. Why?"

He stared at her, his pulse pounding. "Nothing. Forget it."

But he couldn't forget. Not what he saw. Not the Polaroids. Not the blood. Not the gang bang.

Not the way she smiled at him.

The next morning was quiet. Too quiet.

They didn't talk about the dream. They didn't talk about the giant.

They hiked for an hour in silence.

At the top of a hill, Nick stopped to piss behind a tree.

As he zipped up, he noticed a torn piece of fabric snagged on a branch.

Black. Lacy.

He pulled it free and stared.

Panties.

Robin's.

From yesterday?

But she'd had them on when she dressed again.

Hadn't she?

"Robin?" he called.

She appeared around the bend, her shorts hugging her curves, sweat already darkening the fabric between her thighs.

"What?"

"These yours?" he asked, holding them up.

Robin froze. Her face blanked.

Then she looked at the panties.

Then back at Nick.

"No," she said. Too fast.

He frowned. "You sure?"

"Not mine."

And she walked on.

Nick stood still, the panties in his hand, his skin crawling.

He shoved them in his pocket.

After hiking for a good while, they stopped again to rest near a rock outcrop where the wind whistled like a flute. The incline of this last section of the trail was a tad daunting.

Robin sat cross-legged, drinking from her water bottle. Her tank top had shifted, and one breast threatened to spill free.

Nick stared. He couldn't help it.

She caught him looking.

"What?" she asked.

"You just..." he shook his head. "You look different."

Robin raised an eyebrow. "Good different?"

He didn't answer.

Because it wasn't just her body.

It was her eyes.

There was something in them now. A shadow. A flicker.

And it looked right back at him.

CHAPTER 6
Eyes in the Trees

They didn't talk much after the panties.

Robin walked ahead, her pace just slightly faster than normal, not enough to call out, but enough to keep Nick in her rearview. Her **fat ass swayed hard in her shorts**, every step a bouncing, hypnotic defiance.

When they were hiking, Robin would build a good lead on Nick. And when she did build a lead, she wouldn't look back since denying the lacy black underwear.

Nick had kept them. Stuffed deep into his backpack like evidence.

He didn't know what pissed him off more—the lie or the way she acted like it didn't matter.

Maybe she was lying. Maybe it *was* hers.

Or maybe something was fucking with them.

The forest had changed. Subtly. The light didn't feel like it was coming from above anymore. The trail had gone from dirt to soft, wet loam. The air buzzed, and every few seconds, Nick thought he saw a shape in the trees—tall, lean, moving slow.

Then gone.

He touched the brass knuckles in his pocket.

"Nick," Robin called ahead, not turning. "We're being followed."

"We are?"

They stopped on a rocky ridge around noon. The sun was bright, but the forest didn't look right. Trees leaned closer. Shadows lingered longer than they should.

Robin sat with her knees drawn to her chest, arms wrapped tight around them. Her tank top clung to her sweat-soaked body, **her tits pushing forward as she hugged herself**, nipples visible in the sunlight.

Nick scanned the trees.

"We need to talk," he said finally.

Robin didn't respond.

"The panties. The dream. The Polaroids. That big ass guy. Something's happening out here."

"No shit," she muttered. "I feel it too."

"What are we walking into?"

Robin finally turned her head. Her blue eyes were darker today.

"You remember that pouch?"

"Yeah."

"That wasn't just some old Cherokee charm. That was a **mojo.** Blood-bound. Probably used in a binding or banishment ritual."

"Then why didn't you say anything?"

"Because I didn't want to scare you."

"Well, guess what? I'm already scared."

She didn't say anything. Just looked away again.

"We need to get the Hell out of these woods, now," Nick scorned.

They got up after their break. They kept walking. The path narrowed. The air felt wet, thick. Like the forest had a mouth and it was breathing all over them.

Then Nick saw it.

A splash of white, tucked between two rocks near the roots of an oak.

Another **Polaroid.**

He crouched and picked it up.

His throat dried instantly.

The image showed **him and Robin**—last night, mid-sex, beside the river.

She was on top, tits out, riding him. His face was tilted up in pleasure.

And **in the background**—

A figure.

The giant.

Same as before. Just standing in the trees, watching.

Robin leaned over his shoulder, saw the image, and froze.

Her breath left her like someone had punched it out of her lungs.

"That's... from yesterday. Who the fuck took the picture? It wasn't the giant, he's in it! And whoever took this was closer to us than he was! How did we not see that guy?"

They stared at it. Stared into their own exposed bodies, captured like prey.

Nick felt the brass knuckles in his pocket again. He wanted to punch something. Someone. But the woods were silent. Still. Watching.

Robin grabbed the photo and stuffed it into her bra.

"Keep moving," she said, her voice hollow.

That night, they camped without fire again. Neither of them slept.

Robin curled against him in the tent but didn't speak. She trembled in her sleep, muttered in Cherokee once, low and desperate.

Nick lay there with a hard-on he couldn't explain. He wasn't turned on. He wasn't excited.

He was just full of pressure. Heat. Tension. Like something wanted out.

He turned over and gritted his teeth.

The dream from the night before crept into the edges of his mind again.

Robin on the stone slab. The blood. The knife.

The music.

And her voice saying *"Let them take me."*

When he woke, there was a smear of dirt across Robin's chest.

It looked like a handprint.

A large one. Bigger than his hand. And Nick's hands were clean.

Nick sat up fast, heart racing. "Robin?"

She blinked awake, confused. "What?"

"Your chest."

She looked down.

The handprint was dark, streaked. Too big to be his.

"I don't remember anything," she said softly.

Her voice trembled. She wasn't pretending this time.

Nick wiped it off with the corner of his shirt. It left a faint outline, like it had soaked into her skin.

They packed quickly and moved fast. No breakfast. No trail mix. Just adrenaline.

Around mid-day, they reached a break in the trees. A wide flat glade, surrounded by crumbling stone totems.

It felt wrong immediately.

Robin slowed.

"What is this place?" Nick asked.

She didn't answer. She walked to the center, staring down at a patch of scorched earth.

"There was a fire here," she said. "A big one. Long ago."

Nick didn't ask how she knew.

He followed her gaze—and there it was.

Another **Polaroid**. Propped up against a flat stone like an offering.

He picked it up.

This time, it showed **Robin**.

Naked.

Alone.

Standing in the exact spot where she was now— hands raised, eyes closed, head tilted back. Her body smeared in mud. Her mouth wide in ecstasy or pain or both.

Robin saw it and stumbled backward.

"I never— I didn't—"

"Is this from a dream?" he asked.

"I don't know," she said, shaking her head. "I don't know what's real anymore."

Nick stepped toward her, touched her arm. She flinched.

"Robin—"

"You want to fuck me again?" she snapped suddenly. "Is that what this is?"

Nick blinked. "What?"

"Every time something gets worse, you get hard. I feel it on your leg. In your sleep. Even now."

He looked down. She wasn't wrong.

"I don't know why," he said honestly. "I don't understand it. There's something about these woods... its crazy what it is doing to my mind, and my body."

Robin stared at him. "Neither do I."

And for a long moment, they just stood there—two people who'd fucked in the wild, loved each other, had a life together, and still didn't know who the fuck the other really was.

That night, after they set camp, Nick stepped away from the tent to piss.

He aimed toward the trees.

And froze.

Eyes.

Dozens of them.

Glowing faintly. Hanging in the darkness like fruit. No faces. No movement. Just eyes.

Watching.

Nick pulled the brass knuckles from his pocket. His hand shook.

One set of eyes blinked.

He backed away.

When he got back, Robin was asleep.

He didn't tell her about the eyes.

And he didn't close his own all night.

Because he knew this wasn't just the woods anymore.

It was **her**.

Something was already inside Robin.

Something spiritual and evil is following them, while simultaneously starting to reside inside of his girlfriend.

And it had a plan.

CHAPTER 7
Trevor

Like Nick, Trevor hated the woods.

They were damp, unpredictable, and full of things he didn't understand. He'd never been much of a hiker, never trusted animals, and absolutely didn't believe in ghosts.

But this shit was starting to get to him.

He trudged up the trail behind Butch and Lane, sweat darkening the pits of his flannel shirt. Butch was a giant of a man, Lane average build. Trevor was built for many things: pro wrestling, bouncing at a bar, drinking contests... but not hiking. His heavy frame wasn't built for elevation. Not like Butch—**a human bear**—or Lane, a Native American who barely made a sound when he walked, even with that damn patch over one eye.

Butch stopped suddenly, raising a hand.

Lane froze beside him.

Trevor wheezed to a halt. "What now?"

Butch didn't answer. He crouched low, pointing at something on the trail ahead.

A footprint.

Bare.

Small.

"Female," Butch muttered.

Trevor leaned over, hands on his knees. "Jesus. You think it's her?"

Butch didn't say it, but they all thought the same thing:

Butch's daughter.

Missing for a week now. Last seen heading into these woods with a group of friends on some spiritual hike. Never came back. Neither did the others.

Except the **photos.**

They started showing up last week.

Polaroids.

One in Butch's mailbox. Another pinned to a tree. One taped to the windshield of Lane's truck.

All of them taken deep in these woods.

Bodies. Some dead. Some mid-sex. Some staring at the camera like they knew it was there.

In the last one, **Butch's daughter was in the background**—blurry, but unmistakable.

Trevor didn't believe in much, but he believed in **what you could see.**

And what he'd seen?

Had made his stomach twist.

They set up camp as the light faded. Butch sharpened his knife by the fire while Lane hung back, half in shadow, smoking something strange from a little carved pipe.

Trevor sat on a rock, munching trail mix and watching the flames.

"You really think those two sex freaks did it?" he asked finally.

Butch looked up. "They know something. That girl—Robin? She's not just some random hiker. She's part Cherokee. Lane can tell"

"How do you know what their names are, Butch?" Lane asked."Those dirty freaks cry out each other's name when they fuck in plain view for anyone to see. What's the matter with those people?" Butch laughed.

"What does it matter that's she is Cherokee or not?" asked Trevor.

Butch leaned in, eyes hard. "She knows the legend. Spearfinger. Shape shifter. Forest witch. Eats children. Obsidian finger like a razor blade. Eats human liver. Can levitate boulders and chuck them. Downs trees. Almost indestructible. Her only weakness is in her hand- that's where she hides her heart."

"So stupid," Trevor mumbled.

Lane exhaled smoke in a slow stream. "You sound like my uncle. He used to talk about her too. Said she could walk in dreams. Wear someone's skin like a shirt."

Trevor scoffed. "Guys... are you really buying into that?"

"No," Butch said. "But I'm buying into **them**."

He nodded toward the woods. Somewhere out there, Robin and Nick were camped. Hiking the same trail. Maybe even watching them.

"Someone's planting those Polaroids," Butch muttered.

"And those sex freaks are public enemy number one. And we're gonna find out what they've done to my daughter."

Trevor couldn't sleep.

Too many thoughts. Too many noises.

He rolled out of his sleeping bag and stepped away from camp to take a leak. The forest was loud with crickets and wind—but underneath, he heard something else.

A low thrum. A rhythmic slap. Like skin on skin.

He frowned.

It was coming from beyond the ridge.

He should've turned back. Should've zipped up and gone straight to bed.

But instead, he crept toward the sound.

The clearing was just past the stone arch—the one they'd passed earlier and avoided.

Trevor dropped low behind a fallen log and looked through the ferns.

And his jaw dropped.

Robin.

Naked. A goddess. Glowing in the moonlight. **Riding Nick like a demon.**

Her dreadlocks slapped her back with every bounce. Her tits—huge, heavy, perfect— clapped in rhythm. Her mouth hung open, eyes wild, lost in the act.

Nick lay on his back, hands clutching her ass, **his cock disappearing inside her** with every thrust.

They were loud. Animal. Primal. Calling each other's names. Yup. Robin and Nick for sure.

Trevor couldn't move.

His cock twitched in his pants.

Then he saw something behind them.

A face.

Not Butch. Not Lane.

Just… eyes. Pale and unblinking. A feminine shape, standing in the trees, half-shadowed.

Watching.

Trevor blinked—and it was gone.

He scrambled back, breath short, dick still hard, heart racing. Butch was missing. Weird.

Trevor didn't sleep at all that night.

When he returned to camp, he didn't tell Butch what he saw.

Not the sex.

Not the woman in the trees.

Not how his mouth went dry and his cock stayed hard long after the image burned into his brain.

Instead, he sat in silence until the sun rose, staring at the edge of the trees.

The next day, Lane found something nailed to a tree.

Another Polaroid.

He pulled it down and turned it toward Trevor and Butch.

Trevor almost threw up.

It was him.

Watching.

Caught in the ferns. Half-crouched. Mouth open. Eyes locked on Robin's naked body as she rode Nick like a possessed spirit.

Butch stared at the photo.

"What the fuck is this?"

"I don't know," Trevor lied.

Lane grinned. His one good eye gleamed. "Looks like someone's got a front row seat."

Butch said nothing. Just stared at Trevor.

Then he pocketed the Polaroid and walked ahead.

They hiked in silence.

Trevor kept seeing that pale figure in the trees. **Female. Black eyes. One long finger...** Mouth too wide.

He didn't say a word.

But he started to believe.

Not in Nick. Not in Robin.

In this forest's magic.

Because no human being was taking those photos.

CHAPTER 8
The Whispering Woods

Lane didn't tell the others when it started.

He kept it quiet. Like a secret between him and the trees.

The first whisper came just before dawn. He'd been awake, staring at the stars through the canopy, when something hissed from the woods:

"Lane…"

Low. Soft. Like breath through a bone flute.

He sat up, heart thudding.

Trevor was snoring. Butch was sharpening a blade in silence. Neither of them had flinched.

Lane scanned the trees, one hand tightening around the hilt of his knife.

But there was nothing.

Just the woods, breathing around him.

The next whisper came at midmorning.

"She sees you."

It came from behind a stump. Then from up in the branches. Then from somewhere beneath the leaves.

Lane stopped walking. Butch turned, annoyed.

"You good?"

Lane nodded.

But he wasn't.

He wasn't good at all.

Because the voice wasn't just calling to him now.

It was **inside** his head.

They stopped for lunch at a rocky ledge. Butch and Trevor passed jerky back and forth while Lane sat apart, chewing slow, staring at the trees.

The wind had a rhythm to it now. A pulse.

"Lane**…**" it whispered.

"**Come closer…**"

Lane stared down the path. He didn't know why, but he knew—**she was near.**

Butch glanced at him. "You look like hell."

Lane said nothing.

Just listened.

Later that afternoon, they found another Polaroid.

Stuck in the cleft of a tree. Waiting.

Trevor pulled it out.

They all leaned in.

This one showed a **tent**—half-zipped, surrounded by moss and branches.

Inside, barely visible in the shadows, two naked bodies tangled together.

Robin and Nick.

But the photo was wrong.

Because **their eyes were open.**

And they were staring at the camera. Smiling.

Trevor stepped back. "Nope. Nooope. That's some Ring shit right there."

Butch grabbed the photo and stuffed it in his pocket.

Lane said nothing.

Because he hadn't just seen the photo.

He'd **heard it.**

A whisper behind the image.

"Come to us."

That night, Lane couldn't sleep.

The wind had stopped. The animals were quiet. Even Trevor's snoring had died out.

But the **voice** was still there.

"She's close…"

He rose slowly and slipped out of camp, careful not to wake the others.

The trees made no sound under his feet.

His body moved on its own.

He passed stones, roots, strange carvings he didn't recognize. A spiral made of teeth.

And then he saw it.

Robin.

Standing naked in the stream, her back turned, dreadlocks wet and hanging low. Her arms out. Her **thick ass slick with water**, thighs glistening in moonlight.

He froze.

Her voice floated back.

"Come here, Lane."

He didn't move.

"I've been waiting for you."

She turned—**but it wasn't Robin.**

Not really.

Her face shifted.

Eyes too wide.

Teeth too sharp.

Her body stayed perfect—**huge tits, narrow waist, hips made to ride**—but her eyes held something that wasn't human. The way she moved, hypnotizing, alluring, animalistic, almost irresistible. Almost.

He stumbled back.

She took a step towards him in the stream, water running between her thighs.

She looked down at the water lapping against her pussy. She looked up smiling at Lane.

"Aren't you thirsty?" she purred.

Lane turned and **ran**.

Branches whipped his face. Roots clawed his legs. The forest groaned. Nearly blind, he started to panic and hyperventilate as he ran.

Behind him, the whispers rose to a chant:

"Let her in. Let her in. Let her in."

He didn't stop running until he reached camp.

Trevor and Butch jolted awake as he burst in, wild-eyed, bleeding from the arms.

"What the fuck?" Trevor shouted.

Lane dropped to his knees, panting.

Butch grabbed his shirt. "What did you see?"

Lane shook his head. "It wasn't her."

"What?"

"It wasn't that chick with the dreads. Not... not really. It wore her shape. It spoke with her voice."

"What the fuck are you rambling about, dude?" Trevor asked.

Butch's face went pale.

"You saw Spearfinger."

Lane didn't respond.

But the whisper did.

Inside his skull.

"Now you know."

CHAPTER 9
The Thing Inside Us

They were filthy.

Days of sweat, grime, blood, and sex baked into their skin. Robin's tank top was stiff with dried river water and whatever else had leaked from her pores. Nick's T-shirt was crusted in old mud and smelled like sap and old adrenaline.

And still—they couldn't stop looking at each other.

They stopped walking in silence. Just... stopped. Like their bodies had made the decision for them.

"Um..." Robin stood erect, tits straight out, ass sticking out like it was sending a message. She looked down at the forest floor to the side and bit her lip.

A crooked birch leaned like a sentinel over a flat patch of moss and dirt. They dropped their packs, stood there breathing hard, not talking, not blinking.

Something was **building** inside both of them.

It wasn't lust.

It was **pressure.**

Thick. Hot. Magnetic.

Like something buried in the woods was reaching through the ground and **pulling their spines toward each other.**

Robin, wide-eyed, stepped out of her boots slowly, then stripped off her tank top, exposing her **big, perfect tits**, already hard from the cold.

Her hands went to the waistband of her shorts.

And she looked at Nick.

Dead in the eyes.

No words. No smile. Just a silent challenge.

She peeled the shorts down slowly—**inch by inch**, and turned slightly to show off. Exposing her **fat, perfect ass rising like the moon** from beneath the elastic. It jiggled, flexed, settled heavy as she stepped out of them.

She turned away, still naked, and walked to the edge of their clearing.

Then she **got on all fours.**

Didn't look back.

Didn't speak.

Her knees spread. Her back arched. Her **ass lifted high** into the air like an offering.

And she stared into the woods like the Great Sphinx.

Silent. Waiting. Ready to be ridden.

Nick didn't move for a full ten seconds.

Then the thing inside him took over.

He didn't just walk.

He **stalked** toward her, cock already hard, pulsing. Something made him step out of his shorts. He approached this statuesque goddess's willing flesh with a massive erection that was cutting it's way through the damp air.

He dropped to his knees behind her, hands trembling.

His eyes rolled back into his head. Literally—**gone white, like something else had taken the wheel.**

He grabbed her hips with great force. Her ass was slick with sweat and dew.

He stared at it like it was the only thing that mattered in the world.

Round. Heavy. Bouncing already just from the tremble in her thighs.

His cock throbbed—**thick, veiny, flushed with blood.** The head glistened, swollen, leaking pre-cum.

He ran it between her cheeks, teasing the entrance. Robin gasped—then moaned like a beast.

Her face was still turned toward the trees.

She said nothing.

Just waited.

Wanted.

He thrust into her in one brutal motion.

Her body jolted. Her breath caught.

Then she **moaned. Loud. Unnatural. Like something speaking through her.**

Nick slammed into her again. She was sopping wet already. She wanted this. Then again. The sound of his hips hitting her ass echoed off the trees.

He grabbed two fistfuls of her dreadlocks and yanked.

Hard.

Like reins.

She arched, her back taut, moaning louder now.

"Harder," she rasped. "Ride me like a fucking animal."

Nick growled. Actually growled.

He blacked out. They were animals fucking in the woods. Their positioning, their posture, the sounds... the mutual force. When he would slam into her wet pussy, she slammed herself back on the hardest cock she ever felt. Riding her, dreadlocks in hand, otherworldly sex.

He yanked again—**so hard a dreadlock extension tore free.**

Robin screamed.

But her ass didn't stop moving.

She met every thrust with her own. Grinding. Bucking.

Nick's cock disappeared into her with every stroke—**balls slapping, thick shaft pulsing inside her wet heat.**

Robin started crying.

Tears streamed down her cheeks.

"I hate this," she sobbed. "I fucking hate this. What is happening to me?"

But her ass kept bouncing.

Her body refused to stop.

Nick leaned over her back, biting her shoulder. His cock plunged in deeper, faster.

His eyes were still rolled back.

He was **gone.**

Taken.

Possessed.

Robin's hands clawed the dirt.

She moaned. Screamed. Bit her lip so hard it bled.

The forest watched.

Somewhere nearby, a twig snapped.

But they didn't care.

They couldn't.

They were **too deep inside it.**

They wanted everyone to see. Their friends, strangers, their parents, their exes. Watch us fuck. Learn.

THIS IS HOW YOU FUCK, YOU IDIOTS.

When they came, it was simultaneous.

Their yells echoed through the forest for what sounded like miles.

Nick buried himself to the hilt, shouting into the sky as **his cock throbbed**, shooting inside her with wave after wave of raw, primal release.

Robin cried out, her legs shaking, **tits swinging wildly beneath her**, body shuddering with every pulse.

Then they collapsed.

Her face hit the dirt.

He rolled off her.

Panting.

Sweating.

Spent.

Robin curled into herself. Her eyes wide. Wet.

"What… what the fuck was that?" she whispered.

Nick didn't answer.

He was staring at his hand.

Still clutching her **torn dreadlock.**

"You were moaning," he mumbled. "You told me to—"

"I didn't," she said. Her voice trembled. "I didn't say that. I don't remember saying that."

She pulled her knees to her chest. **Her body filthy. Bruised. Her nipples scraped raw from the forest floor.**

"You hurt me."

The words hung in the air.

Nick looked at the spot where they'd just fucked.

At the impression of her knees in the dirt.

At the **slippery trail of fluids between her thighs.**

He wanted to say sorry.

But something inside him whispered:

"Good boy."

CHAPTER 10
The Kings of the Woods

Jude Voodoo adjusted his collar for the millionth time and cursed the Smoky Mountain humidity.

"This ain't no kinda weather for rhinestones and leather," he muttered, slapping a mosquito off his neck. "If I die in this jumpsuit, you tell 'em to bury me facedown, so they can kiss the King's ass."

Jude was an aging Elvis Impersonator, but he was still popular in the tourist town of Pigeon Forge, TN. He even had his own theater back in the 90s.

Behind him, THE **Charlie Hodge** waddled along behind Jude with a duffel bag slung over one shoulder and a stained towel hanging from the other. He was the original Elvis's towel man, handing the King of Rock N Roll scarves and towels onstage for years. But those days, of course, are long gone. But Charlie has befriended Jude over the years. They've been friends for so long, Charlie pretty much treats him like the real Elvis Presley.

"You shoulda wore the yellow vines," Charlie said. "The one with the vents in the sleeves. I told you. You sweat through this one, you're gonna chafe. You're gonna stink. Leather's not breathable, king."

"I will set this whole forest on fire if you bring up costume ventilation or towels again."

Charlie ignored him, as usual. He stepped over a tree root and looked around.

"Y'know," he said, "there's more kinds of towels than most people realize. There's beach towels. Bath towels. Hand towels. Gym towels. Microfiber towels. Suede towels—though those don't absorb worth a damn. Golf towels. Dish towels. Bar towels—oh, them're good for sweat. Good ol' terry cloth."

Jude groaned. "If God was real, he would've struck you with lightning in the first two secondss of that list, baby."

Charlie shrugged. "Jesus used towels. Look it up."

They'd been hiking in circles for at least three hours. Jude's sequined jumpsuit—white, red, and gaudy as hell—was now mostly just a soggy fabric prison. His cape dragged through every thorn bush. His wig was crooked. His patience? Nonexistent.

Charlie didn't seem to notice.

Or care.

He had that wide-eyed dumbass serenity Jude had always hated and somehow couldn't live without.

"Charlie," Jude said finally, "are we lost?"

Charlie didn't answer right away. He paused to wipe his face with a towel—light blue, floral-printed, likely stolen from a Motel 6 in 1989.

"Define lost, king" he said.

"As in, we don't know where the fuck we are."

Charlie grunted. "We're not lost. We're exploring."

"Exploring means you have a destination."

Charlie blinked. "No it don't."

"Exploring means **you don't end up dead in a ditch with your nutsack chewed off by possums.**"

Charlie nodded solemnly. "Could use a nutsack towel in that case. Nutsack towels are a real thing, but it's not for what you would think..."

Jude stopped walking.

"I'm gonna bury you with a monogrammed dishrag shoved down your throat."

The woods were quieter than they should've been.

Even Jude noticed.

No birds. No insects. Just the dull crunch of leaves under boots and Charlie's constant towel commentary.

Charlie suddenly stopped.

Jude turned. "What now?"

Charlie was staring at something near the base of a tree.

"What is it?" Jude asked.

Charlie bent down and picked it up.

A **Polaroid.**

He handed it to Jude.

The photo was blurry but unmistakable: a man and a woman—mid-thrust, tangled together on the forest floor. Her face tilted back. His mouth open. Skin pale. Eyes rolled back.

It looked like it had been taken from the bushes.

Jude stared at it, mouth slightly open.

"Wow. She's a hot damn tamale," Jude Voodoo remarked.

"I think that's the girl from the ranger board," Charlie whispered.

"The newest missing one?" Jude asked.

"No. The one with the dreadlocks."

Jude looked closer. "Yup. She's definitely got dreadlocks. And an ass that never stopped. That's one lucky hombre there, boy."

Charlie nodded. "I told you. There is some kind of freaky sex cult wilderness orgy thing happening out here. We're probably walking through somebody's homemade porno set right now."

"I ain't mad at that!" Jude laughed.

They looked around.

The woods were too still.

Jude slipped the photo into his chest pocket.

Charlie pulled a towel from the duffel bag and twisted it in his hands like a security blanket.

"Y'ever get the feeling you're not supposed to be somewhere?" he asked.

"All the time," Jude said. "Usually on stage."

"No, like… the trees don't want us here."

Jude didn't laugh.

Because for once, **he agreed with Charlie**.

Far above them, in the black limbs of an old hemlock, the **raven** watched.

It cocked its head.

Then flew silently into the trees.

Behind it, something else moved.

Something that did not breathe.

CHAPTER 11
Wile E. Coyote

They should've been back at the car by now.

Robin said it first, but Nick had known it for almost a day.

They were walking in circles.

He checked the GPS on his phone again—just a blinking dot. No signal. The trail ahead looked familiar, but that didn't mean anything anymore.

"I don't get it," Robin muttered. "We followed the exact trail markers. We should've passed the creek again. I used to walk these woods alone as a child. I never got lost or scared, not even once."

"I know," Nick said quietly. "I know..."

Robin turned to look at him. "You think we're lost?"

"No," he said. Then: "Yeah. I do."

They stopped walking. The woods were too quiet again. No birds. No bugs. Just the wind shifting in unnatural directions.

Robin sighed and dropped her pack. "I need to rinse off."

Nick opened his mouth to protest, but stopped himself.

She peeled off her tank top and hiking shorts, revealing a **tight colorful bikini** underneath. She adjusted the top, bouncing her tits slightly as she tied it tighter in the back. She reached into her pack and put on a spare pair of small blue jean shorts. Robin was built in such away that even watching her put on clothes was sexual. If it could have, the bikini's fabric would have screamed as it contorted over her cartoonish round curves.

"You packed a bikini?" Nick asked.

She smirked. "I like to feel cute when I rinse my pits."

She didn't wait for a reaction. She grabbed a water bottle and walked behind a thick clump of brush.

Nick sat on a log, rubbing his temples.

His legs ached. His back throbbed. His balls still hurt from earlier. But most of all, he couldn't shake the feeling that **someone else** was hiking with them.

Not just watching.

Moving. Somehow, some way, he felt like something supernatural was happening here. Like someone was shifting the woods around like cheap furniture in an apartment.

Robin was behind a tree, squatting to pee, jeans shorts pushed around her ankles.

The sunlight danced through the branches, flickering across her thighs. Her skin steamed slightly in the heat.

And then, just as she was pulling her shorts up—

She heard Nick call her name.

Only it wasn't Nick's voice. Not exactly.

It was *off.*.

Back at the trail, Nick stood. Something had moved past him.

A flicker.

Then—

Robin.

But not quite.

Same body. Same devilish curves. But this version wore a **long buckskin dress**, fringe swaying along her hips, beads clicking with every step. Her hair looked glossier. Her eyes darker.

She smiled at him, slow and knowing.

"Robin?" he asked.

She giggled.

Her hands slid to her **massive tits slowly**, lifting them through the thin hide of her top. Her fingers played with her nipples as she looked at Nick with bedroom eyes.

Nick blinked. "Why are you dressed like that?"

She tilted her head and giggled again, but then she started looking serious. She was really getting into playing with her breasts... she moaned, and lifted her chin back, eyes closed. Her knees buckled.

She walked backward, deeper into the trees, still fondling her large tits.

Nick followed.

He wasn't thinking.

The forest around him blurred. The sound of leaves faded. The sunlight dimmed even though the sky hadn't changed. All he could see were her **hips**, the slow swing of them under the ancient dress.

She lost him, and he started getting scared. He couldn't see her through the forest's thick canopy.

"ROBIN? ROBIN!!!"

He picked up the pace. He was worried. What was at first a weird, sexy game of hide and seek has become a moment of peril. What if the giant got her? What if the monster got her? He started running—

And then...**nothing.**

No ground.

No step.

Just air.

Nick realized too late that the trail had ended.

He was walking off a cliff.

He started to drop. He flailed and reached back for anything he could grab onto—caught a root that was luckily sticking out of the cliff face. He scrambled, dirt falling in chunks from beneath his boots.

His heart pounded as he rolled onto solid ground, hands shaking.

At the edge, the drop stretched forever. A hundred feet, three hundred feet, maybe more. Sharp rocks below.

He looked up.

Robin—**the fake Robin**—stood hovering in the air. Out in open space. Her devilish smile gleamed.

She knew Nick was putty in her hands already. So easily manipulated. Men were so easy. She laughed, a horrible, **howling laugh**, sharp as obsidian.

Then she vanished.

Several minutes passed as Nick tried to make his way back to the trail. Running through thorn bushes, tree branches, sticker bushes, poison ivy and the like as he barreled through the line like a fullback in football. Head down... panicking. He didn't care, he almost died but he had to check on Robin. He somehow made it to the main trail and collapsed on it.

Robin found him on his back, panting, covered in sweat and dirt.

"What happened?!"

"I thought I saw you," he said. "You were wearing something different. Old. Native. You were…"

Robin's eyes narrowed.

"You followed her?"

"I didn't know it wasn't you."

"Until when?"

"Until I almost fell off of a fucking cliff."

Robin blinked, "She led you to a cliff…"

"She wanted me dead."

"Oldest trick in the book. And she's not done yet," Robin said, voice low. "Not by a long shot. Oh my God… I can't believe you fell for that. Was she rubbing her tits and you chased her down? Couldn't help yourself? I can't believe this is happening. Men are so… so stupid! God! This is bad Nick, this is real real bad."

"I thought it was you!"

Nick sat up for a few moments catching his breath. Eventually, she extended her hand down to pull him up. They hiked in silence for another hour.

No trail markers. No creek. No car.

Just woods.

The trees didn't repeat—but they all looked the same.

And sometimes… **they looked like they were shifting.**

By late afternoon, they gave up finding the trail that leads to the parking lot and started looking for signs of human life.

A ranger station. A fire tower. A cabin.

Anything.

"I'm not sleeping in these woods again," Robin muttered, still wearing her bikini top and shorts. Her **cleavage gleamed with sweat**, and her thighs were covered in scratches.

Nick tried not to look.

Tried not to want her again.

But that **pressure**... it was coming back. The forest's spell. Plus he was still aroused earlier by evil Robin's tricks.

But they found something just before dusk.

A sign. Wooden. Split in half.

Only one word still legible:

"Station."

They followed the arrow.

And walked straight into a wall of vines.

Behind it, half-buried in the brush, was a crumbling structure—stone and wood, iron bars covering broken windows, and yet the front door was open.

"Ranger station," Nick whispered.

Robin stepped forward.

And from the roof... something moved.

Robin froze. Nick stepped in front of her instinctively.

A long shape—thin, jointed—crawled back over the peak of the ranger station's roof and disappeared with a scraping sound, like fingernails over tin. Neither of them moved for a moment.

"Probably a raccoon," Nick lied.

"Maybe," Robin said. "Or maybe she's watching again."

They pushed through the open doorway together.

Inside, the air was heavy with rot and mildew. A caved-in desk slouched in one corner. The floor was soft and mossy in places, with vines and other types of flora growing up through the slits in the floor. A faded map of the forest was presented on the wall—but it was useless. Most of it water-damaged and peeling.

Robin walked to the desk, brushing cobwebs aside, and picked up a laminated folder that had been chewed on by rodents. Inside were incident reports, ranger notes, and a faded logbook that ended mid-sentence:

"...*no sign of the three hikers reported missing— though photos continue to appear around...*"

Robin dropped it.

Nick picked up a Polaroid from under a collapsed file cabinet.

He turned it over slowly.

It was **himself**—asleep in the tent. Mouth open. Shirt off.

Robin beside him, also asleep, her arm thrown across his chest.

The camera's angle? **From inside the tent.**

Nick felt his stomach lurch. "Someone was in there with us..."

Robin took the photo, stared, then placed it face-down on the desk.

"Let's see if there's a radio or anything."

There wasn't. Besides someone or something planting these Polaroids here, the station had been dead a long time.

But in the back room—through a splintered door—they found something else.

A mattress on the floor. Moldy. Indented.

And **more Polaroids.**

Scattered across the room. Taped to the walls. Hundreds of them.

Most were faded, water-damaged. But a few were new. Crisp.

A woman pinned to a tree.

A man screaming in the rain.

A child's shoe floating in a stream.

Nick and Robin kissing. Naked. Nick's hands on her ass.

Robin, alone. Crying. Covered in something black.

Robin touched one of herself and recoiled. "I don't remember this."

"Because it hasn't happened yet," Nick said.

She looked at him.

They both knew he was right.

Outside, the wind kicked up suddenly—hard and sharp, like a scream. The ranger station creaked. Something clattered across the roof. The wind picked up outside. Unnatural. Violent.

The door slammed shut behind them.

CHAPTER 12
The Hiding Place

The door wouldn't open.

Robin shoved her shoulder into it again, grunting. It didn't budge. From the outside, something had pulled it tight into the frame—twisting the hinges until they screamed.

"We're locked in," she said. Not panicked. Not yet. But her voice was rising.

"Let me try," Nick said.

He braced one boot against the wall and pulled with both hands. The handle creaked, the wood groaned, but nothing gave.

Robin stepped back. "Windows?"

They were broken, yes—but barred. The iron lattice behind them was rusted and overgrown, like the forest had slowly woven itself into the building and wouldn't let go.

They were sealed in.

The ranger station was a box.

And the woods were the lid.

They spent an hour trying every exit, trying to invent new exits. Robin even crawled into the fireplace to check the flue—came out coughing, covered in ash and dead leaves.

"There's no way out," she muttered. "No fucking way."

Nick checked the map again, hoping for anything. The same soggy forest outline. A red arrow pointing to nothing. Worthless.

He shoved it away.

Robin paced.

She was still in her **bikini top and shorts**, body streaked with sweat and soot, her legs scratched from brush, her cleavage rising and falling with shallow breaths.

Nick kept catching himself staring. Goddamn. He was scared as hell and still turned on just by the look of her.

Later, they sat on opposite sides of the station.

Robin picked up Polaroids from the floor and started to arrange them out of boredom. One showed her sitting in the ranger station—right here, right now, doing this very thing—but crying.

Another showed Nick asleep, sprawled on the floor.

A third: the two of them, holding hands, walking into what looked like a cave.

Robin didn't remember that. Neither did he.

"What really scares me, and I'm scared by a fuck ton of things right now, is how some of the Polaroids look like they are predicting the future," she said.

Nick nodded slowly. "Or whatever these things are... is just showing us what it wants to happen."

She looked at him. "Maybe both."

Sometime near sunset, Nick found the loose floorboard.

He stepped wrong, nearly fell through. The plank tilted. Beneath it: a hollow space.

He crouched, pried the board up, and reached inside.

His fingers brushed something smooth. Plastic. Cold.

He pulled it out.

A ziplock bag. Inside it: a **cassette tape**, an old **pocket recorder**, and a half-melted disposable camera.

"Jesus," he muttered.

Robin came over fast. "What is it?"

"It's an old mini tape recorder, the kind lawyers and authors used to use back in like the 80s."Nick reached in the opening again to check and see if anything else was down there. Then he found it. Big, clunky, cold to the touch. He pulled it up from it's wooden grave and Robin and Nick both gasped.

A Polaroid camera. Was it... the Polaroid camera?

"I'm not really interested in touching that magic camera of death, Robin. Do you object?""I agree, man. Fuck that camera." Robin said.

Nick kicked the Polaroid device back into the hole, like it had evil ju ju or cooties all over it.

It fell back into the crawlspace with a plastic thud.

Nick's attention went back to the old cassette recorder. He hit play.

The recorder hissed. Then:

"Day 3. Station's sealed. We've lost the trail. Katie says she saw something in the mirror—wearing her face but not her eyes. I believe her now. I'm sorry I didn't before. I think it's using us."

The tape clicked.

Nick stared at it like it might start speaking again. He fiddled with it, for a few seconds. Removing the tape, blowing on it, wiping the recorder off with his T-shirt. He revealed his abs when he did this, and Robin caught a glimpse. His flat stomach, his bulge and the roundness of his ass contorting his shorts from two directions. Why was she thinking about that now? There's no time for any of that. Plus, they are both disgusting and in great need of soap. And she is frightened. Still, all she could think about for a few moments was his cock in her mouth. "Mmmmmm... Stop that, freak," she thought. She diverted her eyes to the floor.

Nick hit play again. This time it worked. It was the sounds of a man and woman, fucking. Like animals. They were enjoying it immensely from the sound of things, so much so her cries of pleasure were shorting out the little recorder's mic. The tape stopped again.

Nick didn't move his eyes, "No matter how scared they were..."

Robin finished the thought, "They just had to fuck."

Nick and Robin's eyes met. Hers slid up from his ass to meet his eyes, his eventually popped down to her massive chest, and they both could feel it. Whatever was messing with this couple on the tape's labito, was manipulating theirs as well.

That night, they built a fire in the old stone hearth. The room flickered with orange shadows. Robin sat with her legs crossed, arms wrapped around herself.

Something had changed in her.

She hadn't spoken much since the tape. She kept glancing at the shadows on the wall like they might move when her back was turned.

Her voice broke the silence.

"I feel her inside me."

Nick blinked. "What?"

Robin's eyes stayed on the flames. "She's not in my head. She's… lower. Somewhere deep."

"Robin—"

"She watches through my eyes sometimes. I can feel it. And when you look at me like that?" Her gaze turned to him. "I don't know if you're looking at *me* or *her.*"

Nick swallowed hard.

"You!"

But he didn't know if he was lying or not.

They didn't sleep.

The fire burned low. Outside, the woods made new sounds.

Scratching.

On the walls. On the roof. Beneath the floor.

Something was circling.

Just before dawn, Robin got up and walked into the back room.

Nick was curious at his girlfriend's early morning movements. He followed a moment later.

He found her sitting in the corner, legs wide, her bikini top pulled down, fingers to her lips like she didn't want him to speak.

Her eyes were glassy. Her voice was a whisper.

"She wants you."

Nick didn't move.

"She wants you to come over here."

Robin's tits were bare now, glistening in the low light. Her shorts were unbuttoned. Her legs were parted just enough.

Nick stepped closer—then stopped.

"Is this you?"

Robin smiled.

And her voice changed.

Not pitch. Not volume.

Weight.

He'd heard it before.

In the clearing. In the hallucination.

Spearfinger...

CHAPTER 13
Possession

The ranger station was now a tomb with walls.

Nick looked at her on the ground with a stern look. "Snap out of it."

She was beautiful, she was hot. But he wasn't going to fall for this game again. Nick stood up quickly, turned, and went into the next room.

"Fuck this shit."

Robin's mind came back fully. She was embarrassed and covered up. She knew Spearfinger was starting to have more and more control, but Nick's rejection snapped her fully back. At least... mentally.

Robin's whole body felt tight. Buzzing. Not from fear—but from something low in her belly.

The air inside the station had grown humid, thick like syrup. It was hard to breathe. Her skin prickled, sweat slick between her breasts.

"I'm gonna look in the back again," she muttered. "Maybe I missed something. Sorry... sorry about that."

Nick was hunched over the dead shortwave radio, muttering curses. He barely looked up.

Robin slipped into the rear office, the shadows swallowing her.

That's when the temperature dropped.

And the whispers began.

"Robin..."

The voice was like a memory whispered through a dream. It wrapped around her spine, slithered up her neck.

She turned.

And saw herself in the corner.

Standing by the boarded window—barefoot, wild, ancient.

Her hair was the same: dark brown dreadlocks cascading over her shoulders. Her body: identical. But this woman wore no modern clothes. Only a wrap of deerskin, bone beads around her neck, and feathers woven into her hair. Her skin glowed with an inner light. Her eyes were black lakes. She had paint on her face... creating a thick bar across her eyes. She had what looked like black war paint on her chin, three lines pointing up to her big red lips.

Robin's heart thudded.

"What...what are you?"

The woman stepped forward, barefoot on the dusty wood.

"I'm you. I've always been in you," she said, her voice layered—Robin's tone, but deeper, older, cracked by time and secrets.

"No you are not!" Robin whispered, stepping back.

"Yes," the other said. "You've always wanted to know. What it would feel like. A woman's touch. Your own hands on your own body. But better. Raw. Real."

Robin's throat went dry, "Wh-what?"

Her mother's voice echoed in her head. **Sin. Temptation. Lust is the devil's favorite sin.**

She'd grown up Southern Baptist. Tent revivals. Purity pledges. Sunday school. "A woman shall not lie with another as with a man."

But she *had* wondered.

Late at night. Touching herself in secret. Fantasizing about girls in gym class. A substitute teacher once. The female lead in that vampire TV show.

And now she was face to face with herself.

And she wanted her.

The shame shot through her like lightning.

"Fuck," Robin whispered. Her legs trembled. "This is wrong. I- I can't..."

The spirit smiled gently.

"That's why it's good."

She stepped close. Robin didn't move.

"And yes... you can."

They were eye to eye. Breast to breast. The spirit reached out, fingers brushing Robin's cheek.

"You've never kissed a woman, have you?"

Robin shook her head no, like a scared animal.

"You want to."

Robin's jaw clenched. "I can't. I'm not—I'm not a…"

The spirit's lips touched hers. Featherlight. Soft. Then harder. A kiss like no other's. Better than any man she has ever kissed.

Robin whimpered.

It was like kissing herself in a dream. Familiar but forbidden. Her hands rose, meant to push the spirit away—but they clumsily tangled in the leather wrap instead, pulling it loose.

Spearfinger's tits spilled free—perfect. Round. Her nipples dark and tight.

Robin looked down at her perfect breasts and gasped.

"Jesus, help me," she whispered.

But her body had already chosen.

She quickly dropped her bikini top. Her own breasts bounced free, nipples aching.

The spirit cupped them, massaged them. Sucked one into her mouth. Spearfinger looked up playfully, she knew she had won. She owned her.

Robin moaned. Eyes closed. Head tilted towards the ceiling.

Back in the hallway, Nick had paused. He'd been pacing, but now he stood completely still, hearing muffled sounds—moaning, breathing. He crept toward the cracked door.

And froze.

His jaw dropped.

Robin. On the desk. Legs open. Her shorts gone. Her doppelgänger licking her thighs.

Nick felt sick. And hard.

He unzipped, hand trembling.

Inside the office, Spearfinger kissed Robin like they were lovers. Her tongue flicked across Robin's nipples, down her belly. She pulled Robin's leg over her shoulder, kissed her inner thigh, and licked slowly up between her lips.

Tongue on top, two fingers plunged into her folds. Back and forth, back and forth as the tongue rapidly explored her.

Robin screamed—soft and high-pitched. Her back arched. One hand covered her mouth. The other gripped the desk behind her.

The shame was blinding. White-hot. But so was the pleasure.

She'd never felt anything like this. Not with Nick. Not with anyone.

"I'm not supposed to like this," she moaned.

Spearfinger laughed against her pussy. "But you do."

Robin's body was betraying her. Wet. So wet. Her thighs trembled. Her whole body jerked as the spirit circled her clit with inhuman skill.

Back in the hallway, Nick stroked faster, his face twisted in guilt and desire.

Robin came.

Once.

Then again. Harder.

The spirit didn't stop. She kept licking, fingers teasing Robin's ass, squeezing it, spreading it, exploring every inch of her trembling flesh.

Robin sobbed, overwhelmed.

"I'm a sinner," she whispered.

"Then sin harder," the spirit said.

Robin came again. Her body locked up. Her vision blurred.

The spirit stood, tits glistening with sweat, her mouth smeared with Robin's taste. She pulled Robin close and kissed her deeply. Tongues tangled.

"You belong to me now," she whispered.

Robin collapsed against the desk, body twitching, her thighs soaked and sore.

The air shifted.

The front door creaked open.

Nick stumbled into the room, his cock still out, his face pale.

"Robin?"

Spearfinger was gone. Vanished like smoke.

Robin blinked up at him, dazed.

"I—I don't…"

He rushed to her, wrapping her up in his arms.

"You're okay. It's okay."

Robin clung to him, naked and shaking.

"I feel amazing," she said. "I feel…free."

But even as she said it, a cold dread began curling in her stomach.

Outside, the forest wind had changed.

It no longer howled.

It purred.

Like something satisfied.

They dressed in silence, hands trembling. The shame clung to both of them like another layer of sweat. The front door was still open.

Robin glanced back once—at the desk. At the wet spot. At the memory of her own hands touching her own body and another.

Then they fled into the woods together, hand in hand, holding each other too tightly.

And behind them, deep inside the ranger station, something ancient smiled.

CHAPTER 14
Bloom

The forest welcomed them.

After all the screaming, the endless sweat, the crushing paranoia—the silence was gentle now. The leaves no longer whispered. The trees no longer loomed. They swayed. Danced. Welcomed.

Robin and Nick held each other as they walked, trying not to think about the door that had opened by itself, the spirit that vanished like steam, the lingering smell of sex and shame on Robin's thighs.

When they finally stopped, it was in a clearing they hadn't seen before.

It was unreal—like a painting from a place that didn't exist.

Flowers bloomed where there shouldn't be flowers. The glade looked liked a meticulously maintained garden with flowers foreign to this place. A single tree stood in the center, white-blossomed, massive and blooming with out-of-season fruit. The air shimmered like it was laced with heat or pheromones. A raven sat on a branch above, its head cocked, watching them.

Robin stared at the tree, almost hypnotized. She let go of Nick's hand and stepped forward. "It's beautiful," she whispered.

Nick looked around, cautious. "Yeah... and I don't trust it."

"I do," she said, dreamily. "It's calling us."

The raven let out a long, low croak.

Robin slid her shorts down, slowly, sensually. She wasn't wearing underwear. Her ass glowed in the filtered light, round and perfect, still marked faintly by finger-shaped bruises from earlier. Her bikini top was untied, swinging at her sides like a forgotten garment.

She stepped under the tree and lay back in the grass, legs spread, arms stretched over her head. She looked like a goddess—like Eve begging for the serpent.

Nick swallowed. His cock stirred, twitching in his shorts. But his brain was still screaming, What are we doing?

Robin moaned. Not from pain or pleasure. From something deeper. A *need*. A *pull*.

"I want you to fuck me," she said. "Right here. Now."

Nick didn't move. "What? Are you serious?"

Robin arched her back, her hands drifting down to her soaked slit. "Please," she said. "Something inside me… it needs it. I need you to fill me. Stretch me. Claim me back."

The raven flapped its wings once and settled.

Nick dropped his backpack. Walked forward.

"Robin…" he said. "What happened back there… I saw it. I saw you. With—yourself."

She nodded, lips parted. "It was me. It wasn't. I don't know. But it made me feel things I've never felt before. And it's not gone. She's still in me. I can feel her watching. I want her to watch this."

Nick clenched his jaw. He looked at her exposed body—sweat-slicked tits rising with each breath, thighs wet and spread, ass planted in the enchanted grass.

His cock was hard now. He hated that it was.

"This is absolutely crazy, Robin!"

But his mood changed, like something flipped a switch.

He pulled down his pants and stepped between her legs.

As he sank into her, they both groaned.

But the pleasure was *different*. Softer. Sweeter. As if the forest itself was moaning with them. Flowers opened wider. Wind curled around them like breath. The branches swayed rhythmically, matching their thrusts.

Robin looked up and whispered something—too soft to hear.

"What?" Nick asked, fucking deeper now.

"I was thinking of her," she whispered. "When you entered me."

Nick froze.

Robin smiled sadly. "I'm sorry."

He kept moving.

Because he couldn't stop. He hated those words. He wanted to fuck her harder now.

Because some part of him *wanted* her to be thinking of someone else. Because the idea of Robin getting off on her own reflection—on another version of herself—was the most erotic, disturbing thing he'd ever imagined.

Plunge, plunge, plunge...The sex act looked ordinary from the outside, it was the missionary position. But they looked deep into each other's eyes. Robin was crying tears of joy. It was somehow innocent, sweet, like screwing on an Easter morning. And then somehow dirtier, owned, pagan at the same time.

Whatever it was, it was hot as fuck.

The orgasm was slow. Deep. Full-body. Robin cried out like a banshee. Nick grunted and filled her.

When they collapsed together in the grass, the raven finally flew away.

They stayed there for a while, curled against each other under the impossible tree, dozing. The birdsong was melodic. The shadows were long.

Until the wind changed again.

Robin's eyes snapped open. "Do you hear that?"

Nick sat up, immediately on edge. "What?"

She sat up, tits swinging with the motion. "Music."

He blinked. "The fuck?"

And then they saw him.

Emerging from between two black pines—seven feet tall, broad as a barn door, wearing tattered trunks and a cape covered in blood and stickers—**Bestiality**, the wrestler.

A local legend. A myth. A man with an unclean name and a reputation soaked in swamp fights and backwoods pay-per-view, indy wrestling shows, short bits in jail and hidden acts of bestiality with the local livestock of all kinds.

He was shirtless, hairy, coated in dirt and blood, and wore a luchador-style mask stitched from animal hide. A steel folding chair hung from one hand.

He paused when he saw them.

Robin scrambled for her shorts, covering her tits.

Bestiality raised one hand and said, in a soft Southern drawl: "Y'all see the deer that talked in tongues?"

Nick stood. "We don't want any trouble, man."

Bestiality tilted his head. "Trouble ain't up to me no more. Trouble's in the trees. Trouble's in her finger."

He pointed behind them.

Nick turned.

Nothing was there.

When he looked back, Bestiality was gone.

Not walked away.

Gone.

Robin was already crying out. "We have to move."

"Where?"

"I don't know."

They dressed quickly. Everything smelled like rot now. The nearby tree had begun to drip sap that looked like pus. The petals were browning. The grass beneath them twitched.

They ran.

That night they camped near a stream, half-starved and afraid to sleep.

Robin sat with her arms around her knees, staring into the darkness.

"I'm not me anymore," she said.

Nick didn't answer.

"Something's in me," she whispered. "And I like it."

He said nothing.

She looked over. "Are you afraid of me?"

He nodded.

"Me too," she said.

CHAPTER 15
The Whispering

Butch hadn't slept.

He stood at the edge of camp, firelight licking at the side of his face, clutching his daughter's torn hoodie in one fist like it was the only thread holding him together. "EMMA" was scrawled in Sharpie inside the collar—her handwriting. He ran his thumb over it again and again, memorizing the loops. The scent was gone, replaced by something damp and sour.

Behind him, Trevor sat on a log gnawing beef jerky, watching the fire like it might answer something.

"You sure it's hers?" Trevor asked gently.

Butch didn't turn. What a stupid ass question, he thought. "She wore this on the last hike we took. Last spring. She tied it around her waist when she got hot."

"I remember that." Trevor hesitated. "I remember y'all coming back. You were covered in mud."

Butch finally cracked a smile, faint and short-lived. "She took a picture of me. I slipped and faceplanted into a creek bed. She laughed her ass off. Framed the Polaroid. Said it was proof I wasn't immortal."

Trevor chuckled. "Shit, I remember that one. She brought it into the restaurant, showed it to the whole damn kitchen."

Butch glanced over at him. "You were working the line back then, right?"

"Yup. Salad bitch. And you were expo, all high and mighty calling tickets like a drill sergeant."

Butch shook his head, a real laugh catching in his throat this time. "We were assholes."

"We still are."

They sat in silence for a moment, the fire crackling between them.

"Never thought we'd be doing this together," Trevor muttered. "Not here. Not like this."

Butch stared into the dark woods. "I just want her back."

Lane was pacing now, agitated. His eyes were tired. He might have been blind in his milky white eye, but it was still tired. He kept mumbling to himself and wiping his forehead like he was trying to wash away a thought.

"She had a camera," Lane said finally. "Emma. Always had it. Even back when we did that three-day in the Smokies. Remember?"

Butch nodded slowly.

"She got that one of you in the mud. Said it was her favorite photo she ever took."

Trevor leaned forward. "Maybe if we find the camera, we'll find a clue. She might've dropped it near wherever she…"

He didn't finish.

Lane turned suddenly. "I'm gonna take a piss."

Trevor nodded. "Don't go far."

Lane gave a weak wave and disappeared into the trees.

The whispers started as soon as Lane unzipped.

Low. Feminine. Wet.

At first, he thought it was wind.

Then it said his name.

"*Lane…*"

He stiffened. Looked around.

"*She sees you.*"

He grabbed his revealed cock instinctively. Shielding it from spying eyes.

He turned in a slow circle, heart pounding. "Who's there?"

Nothing.

The trees bent slightly, as if something huge had passed through them.

Then the singing began.

A woman's voice. Low. Haunting. Not English. It echoed like a lullaby sung in stone.

Lane didn't even realize he was walking until he was ten paces off trail. The trees thinned. Something glimmered ahead. A feather? What the fuck it that?

The voice whispered again: "*You want to know what she felt.*"

Lane's hand went to his temple. "What who felt? Shut up," he muttered. "Shut the fuck up."

But he kept marching instinctively.

Butch and Trevor went looking for Lane and found his pissing tree about twenty minutes later. But something was different.

Polaroids were pinned to the bark in a spiral. Dozens of them. A blooming wheel of sex and madness.

Robin and Nick.

Naked in a cave. Fucking under a tree. Her bouncing on top of him, tits flailing. One where Nick had his fingers in her mouth while she arched her back and clawed at his thighs. Another where she straddled him in a flooded hallway. Where the hell could that have been?

Trevor stared in stunned silence. "Jesus Christ… These two..."

Butch didn't speak. He was already walking forward, scanning the photos.

In the center of the spiral was a single image. His hand reached out, slow.

It was Emma.

His daughter.

A selfie. Her eyes wide, face dirty. Fear all over her. She was holding her camera up like a shield.

Taped beneath the photo was a scrap of paper.

It read:

THEY MADE ME

Butch's legs nearly buckled. Trevor caught him by the shoulder.

"Oh fuck," Trevor whispered. "Oh fuck, man…"

Butch tore the photo from the tree.

He didn't say anything.

Didn't cry.

Just clenched his jaw until it ached.

Lane returned to camp near sunset.

His pants were wet. His eyes were blank. He sat by the fire and didn't look at either of them.

He started chewing on a stick.

Butch didn't notice.

He was cleaning his knife in silence.

CHAPTER 16
The Elevator

Nick moved past the edge of camp into the dark, damp woods. He didn't say anything to Robin. She was asleep—curled in her bag, legs bare, her dreadlocks fanned across the leaves like a halo. She looked peaceful. Clean. Untouched by the nightmares clawing through his brain.

But his body wasn't peaceful.

His cock throbbed, heavy in his shorts. He has no idea what is happening to his body. Ever since he has been in the forest, he has been erect for what feels like half of the day and half of the night. The littlest thing will set it off, too. Robin flicking her dreads over her shoulder. Looking at her lick her lips. The sway of her goddess-like ass as she walked ahead. A memory. And the sweat, the filth, the heat, the cold... nothing deters it. A raging, purple headed monster is living in his pants. More determined than when he was in puberty. It was like he was living in a twisted commercial for Viagra.

He didn't even try to piss. He just stood with his hand against a tree, breathing hard.

And then, like a trick of heatstroke or haunting—

The forest melted.

And he was back.

Memphis.

The Sheraton elevator.

The lights buzzed. The panel glowed. His gi stuck to his skin, still damp from the final match. The **silver medal**—second fucking place—rested like a scar across his chest.

He was disqualified for trying to break his competitor's neck in a move he saw in pro wrestling, not judo... the surfboard stretch. "If he was in pain, that chump should have tapped!" Nick thought.

It was double elimination, so in the rematch in the finals, Nick tapped like a bitch to a rear naked choke. He was angry and was too pissed off to fight. He didn't even want to be there. He could have used that anger to help him win the state championship, but instead he just quit. Submitted. He wanted to kill the referee from the match before. That's all he could think about.

He hit the button for his floor.

The doors opened.

And they walked in.

Four freaking furries.

Each one surreal. Obscene.

The Fox had glossy orange fur, with a long velvet snout and human shaped tits like overstuffed pillows in a low-cut leather vest. Her bushy tail swayed with every step.

The Wolf wore a pink cheerleader outfit with her legs in pink stockings. White lace garters peeked out beneath the skirt. Her ears twitched. Her paws had pink fingernail polish.

The Cat had a sleek black body suit with a zipper down the front, undone just enough to reveal furred cleavage and he remembered the cat wearing a jingle bell choker around her neck. It kinda glittered like Julie Newmar's Catwoman outfit in the old Batman show.

The Bear stood behind them. Towering. Quiet. His fur was matted. His mask didn't smile—it just stared. He wore nothing but obscenely tight wrestling tights, wrestling boots, and a fake championship belt with the words "A real mother fucker" on it.

None of them spoke.

Then, the Fox leaned against him, her tits brushing his arm. "We watched your matches," she said, voice muffled and soft. "You're strong."

"Apparently not strong enough, weirdos. Get the fuck off of me," Nick muttered, hitting the panel again.

Ding. Nothing.

The Wolf blocked the button. "You move like a predator," she whispered.

The Cat rubbed her cheek against his. "But you smell like prey."

He started freaking out a tad.

The Bear didn't move.

Then the Fox placed her paw flat against his chest and pushed. Just enough to say: "**Stay boy.**"

And to Nick's surprise, he did.

They moved around him like orbiting moons. The Wolf kissed his neck through the fur. The Cat unwrapped the top of his gi, pawing his chest. The Fox tugged loose the cloth belt, exposing his cock.

It was hard.

Already hard.

WHAT THE FUCK?

That was the worst part.

Why? Why now? Why them?

His cock just stuck out there in the air for what seemed like ten seconds. No one did anything. Until...

The Fox gripped him first—stroking, gentle, almost sweet. Her padded hand squeezed the shaft like she was testing the weight of him.

Then the Wolf took over. Her paws stroked his hips, but her real hands freed themselves out of her gloves and snuck up and cupped his balls. She laughed softly. "So full," she whispered.

The Cat knelt behind him and dragged her claws down his spine, traced his ass crack with her finger and then reached underneath and took her turn. Her grip was firmer. Cruel. Curious.

Nick's body shuddered.

What the fuck are you doing?

He told himself to stop.

To speak.

To move.

He didn't.

The strokes came faster. Slower. Back and forth like they'd rehearsed this. His cock throbbed with each pass. His breath was ragged.

They guided him to his knees.

Then to his hands.

All fours, like an animal himself.

He went willingly.

His pants fell from his hips like water. The gi belt lay on the elevator floor—only it wasn't the elevator anymore. The carpet had become moss. The metal, bark. Trees leaned in. Stars blinked above like they were watching.

He moaned.

And hated himself.

The Cat kissed his ass cheek. The Deer fondled his balls from behind. The Fox rubbed his back in circles like he was a child ready for bed.

They took turns stroking him.

Hands on his cock.

On his crack.

On his thighs.

This is so fucking wrong.

But his body begged for more.

And then—the Bear stepped forward.

Massive.

Silent.

His paw wrapped around Nick's cock with **complete authority**.

The stroke was firm. Confident. Not playful.

Nick gasped—because it was perfect.

His hips twitched.

NO.

You're not gay. You're not gay.

And then—

Flashes.

He was **ten**, standing by the pool, watching his cousin's friend pull off his trunks to get into the pool naked for some reason. **The curve of his ass**, round and soft... perfect. He stared too long.

He was **thirteen**, jerking off to a borrowed, severely scratched porno DVD, pretending to watch the girl—but really watching the guy's cock. **Thick. Veiny. Powerful.** He watched it cum three times before realizing he hadn't looked at the woman once.

He was **sixteen**, and dreamed about a boy on the wrestling team. The dream was **soft**—not porn, not lust. Just holding. Just kissing. He woke up hard and sticky and wouldn't talk to the kid for a month.

He buried it.

Deep.

Darker than even Robin could reach.

It didn't mean anything. It was puberty.

It didn't define him.

The Bear leaned down.

His mask brushed Nick's ear.

Stroking, stroking, stroking. The Bear's firm grip was perfect, sliding back and forth on Nick's hard, massive cock in perfect rhythm. Was this the best hand job he's ever had?

His voice was low, rough, soaked in certainty. It was definitely a man in this suit.

"You were always prey, gay boy."

And Nick exploded.

The orgasm ripped through him like a scream with no mouth.

Cum hit the moss. His stomach. His hands.

His entire body twitched.

He wanted to die.

He wanted to come again.

The Bear didn't stop stroking.

The Fox petted his hair like he was hers.

The Wolf whispered, "Good boy."

And the Cat kissed the small of his back.

He stayed there—on all fours, panting, dripping, drained.

Owned.

He blinked—and the world snapped.

He was in the woods.

The real woods.

Face in dirt. Hands muddy. Pants still down. His cock twitching in the cold breeze. Ass up in the air.

Sticky.

Silent.

Then a voice behind him.

"Nick…?"

He flinched.

Robin.

Standing a few feet away, half-dressed, confused, horrified.

He yanked up his pants and turned from her.

"Don't," he said.

"What—what just happened?"

"Nothing."

"You said something. About a boy."

"It wasn't real."

She stepped closer, hesitating.

"Was it… about you?"

His jaw clenched.

"It was the woods, a weird hallucination. It's done. That's all. The witch is playing games again. She won't stop!"

Robin didn't speak again. She didn't press.

She just watched him for a long, quiet moment.

And somewhere in the trees, a **raven** let out a long, low caw—like laughter too old to understand.

CHAPTER 17
The First Kill

Charlie Hodge was tired of the woods.

His polyester outfit was soaked through, sticking to his chest like a used napkin. His boots were caked in red clay. His shoulder hurt from lugging a giant bag of towels, a thermos, and a plastic bag of turkey jerky he'd been rationing for the past four hours.

Worst of all, **Jude Voodoo was missing.**

"Jude!" he called, voice cracking. "Come on, man! You're freakin' me out!"

Nothing answered but the wind.

Trees groaned overhead. Leaves twisted in slow, unnatural spirals, like they were reacting to something **unseen**.

Charlie wiped his forehead with a **navy towel**, then tucked it into his belt. He didn't like this. Not one bit. The trail had vanished behind him, swallowed by moss and shadow. The sun was gone. Not set—**gone.**

Something rustled behind him.

He turned. "Jude?"

Silence.

Then—singing.

Low. Female. Not English. Repetitive.

A soft, slow melody that crawled across the air like it had been waiting just beneath the surface of the forest.

"Nope," Charlie whispered, backing up. "Nope, nope, nope— KING? WHERE ARE YOU KING?"

The singing grew louder.

He spun—

And saw her.

Spearfinger.

Tall. Elegant. Terrible. The sexiest thing he has ever seen. Better than any Elvis groupie by a mile.

Her long brown dreadlocks hung wet and gleaming over bare shoulders. Her skin shimmered like granite, and her face—somewhere between beautiful and **wrong**—was calm and unreadable.

She floated forward, not walking, her feet inches above the ground.

One hand hung loose at her side, fingers long—one of them longer than all the rest. **Jet black. Obsidian.** Like a knife forged in the belly of the mountain.

The raven flapped into view, landing on a branch above her. It cawed once. Low. Final.

Charlie dropped the towel.

"Oh shit—oh shit oh shit—"

He turned.

And ran.

Branches clawed at his arms. Roots tried to trip him. The woods blurred around him, too dense, too dark. He didn't look back. He didn't need to.

He could **feel** her behind him.

Floating.

Singing.

The raven followed like a second shadow, wings slicing the air without flapping.

Charlie's breath came in ragged bursts. His chest burned. His legs ached. He tore through bramble and ducked under limbs, heart pounding like it was trying to escape his chest.

He stood there, trembling. Clinching a towel like it was an old friend. He started nervously singing,

"don't be cruel... to a heart that's true... don't be cruel... to a heart—"

Then—**a sound**.

The air changed.

Heavy.

Wrong.

Charlie skidded to a stop just in time to see the boulder rise.

It was the size of a grill, smooth and black with moss streaked across one edge.

It floated six feet in the air.

Spinning slowly.

Charlie screamed. He turned to run.

And the boulder launched—

Crack.

The sound echoed like a gunshot.

It hit Charlie square in the back of the skull.

His body flew forward, flipped once, and landed hard.

Dead silence.

Spearfinger floated over the fallen man.

His body twitched once, then went still.

She tilted her head, observing the shape of him. She sang quietly as she descended, her bare feet never touching the ground.

The raven landed beside her and croaked once.

She extended her long, obsidian finger and traced a line down Charlie's back, splitting it perfectly like a doctor's scalpel.

Then, after examining the insides of Charlie Hodge, she slowly, reached under his ribs, and began to **pull.**

The finger didn't slice—it **slid**, like a hot needle through wax.

She separated the organs with gentle precision, humming to herself.

Charlie's eyes flickered once. His mouth twitched.

Still alive.

Barely.

Spearfinger leaned close and whispered, "You're lucky."

She slid the finger deeper and began **stretching** the liver.

Not tearing. Not yanking.

Stretching—inch by inch, drawing it out like taffy.

Charlie gurgled.

His hands twitched weakly against the dirt.

Blood pooled beneath him, soaking into the soil.

The raven cawed again.

She smiled as she **fed.**

Mid meal she observed the pooling blood around Charlie.

"Oh no, let me get that."

She reached into Charlie's nearby duffle bag, pulled out a green towel with yellow roses and threw it on the pooling blood.

She chuckled. The raven cawed.

Half a mile away, Jude Voodoo was frozen in place.

He hadn't moved in five minutes.

He'd heard something—**not a scream**, but worse. A sound like **stone hitting meat**. Then the singing again.

It was closer now.

He turned in a slow circle, one hand resting on the pistol tucked in the side of his rhinestone jumpsuit.

"Charlie…" he whispered.

He didn't run.

Not yet.

But he knew.

He was alone now.

And something was coming for him.

CHAPTER 18
The Cave

Robin and Nick moved through the trees like ghosts—sweaty, scraped, covered in dirt. Every step squelched. Every branch grabbed. The silence of the forest was too perfect, like the woods were holding its breath.

It was late afternoon, but the sun had vanished behind a wall of green. Light filtered down in sickly stripes. Somewhere far off, a raven called once—then again. Louder. Closer.

Nick's brass knuckles were out.

Robin trudged ahead, her tank top clinging to her back, her shorts dark with grime. Her legs were smeared with scratches. Her hair stuck to her neck. She looked incredible. She looked wrecked.

He watched her ass sway with each step and hated himself for getting hard again. What is happening? He thought.

She glanced back, catching his look.

"You're quiet," she said.

Nick didn't answer.

She slowed her steps until they were walking side by side.

"You're mad," she said.

Still nothing.

She sighed. "If you're mad about what happened in the ranger station…"

"I'm not mad," he snapped.

"Then what?"

He exhaled through his nose, jaw clenched. "I keep seeing you. With her. With… yourself. It was hot. But it—messed me up."

Robin raised an eyebrow. "You're jealous?"

Nick stared straight ahead.

"You're jealous I had sex with me?"

"It wasn't you. It was... a monster. I don't know what the fuck I am," he muttered. "You were possessed. But you also… liked it."

Robin stopped walking. "Yeah. I did."

He turned, lips parting.

"I liked the way she touched me. I liked how it felt. I liked cumming like I was being split in half. And I'm not sorry. I never felt like that before in my life."

Nick flinched like she slapped him.

Robin took a step closer. "You're the one who watched. Jerking off in the corner. So don't give me the righteous act now."

He looked away.

She smirked. "And I wasn't the one on all fours getting my cock stroked by a bear in a fursuit."

Nick's head snapped back to her.

Robin's smile faded.

"I heard you," she said quietly. "You said 'gay boy.' Loud."

Nick's face turned hard. "That wasn't real."

"It looked real to me," Robin said, stepping past him.

Then she froze.

Stopped cold.

Nick almost walked into her.

She was staring into the trees.

"What—?"

He followed her gaze.

Butch.

Standing maybe thirty feet away.

Unmoving.

Watching.

His flannel was half-unbuttoned. He wasn't hiding.

He wasn't trying to.

Robin whispered, "Run."

They ran.

The cave wasn't far.

Just a jagged crack in the side of a hill, barely taller than their shoulders, but deep and dark and safe enough. Or so they thought.

They ducked inside and collapsed, panting, their backs to the cold stone.

"I think he saw us," Nick said.

Robin laughed, breathless. "You think, dumbass?"

They sat in silence for a moment, breath rising like smoke in the gloom. The cave smelled like wet stone, rust, piss, and something worse.

Guano.

The walls were streaked with it. Shiny. Black. Sticky.

Bat shit.

Robin's lips parted. "It stinks in here."

"Yeah," Nick said, wiping sweat from his face. "Perfect place for a honeymoon."

Robin turned to him. Her eyes were different now—hungry. Wild.

She smiled a strange smile.

"I can't believe you jerked off watching me get fucked by a nasty old forest witch."

"I told you, there's something crazy going on inside of us. I'm like hyper-sexual right now. Like under a spell or something. I'm not taking any of this sex stuff happening in these woods too serious right now. We can talk about it later. It's like... something is bending our wills."

"Is that right, funny man? You aren't taking anything too serious?" She started shifting side to side.

He noticed a change in her personality and demeanor. "Uh oh... now what?"

She reached over and wiped guano off of the cave wall. It was on her hand. She held it up to show Nick.

"Don't— What the--- Robin that is bat shit, don't get that on me, I swear to-" Nick started.

She looked down at her exposed cleavage. She smeared it across her chest.

Across both tits.

Then down her stomach.

Nick's jaw dropped.

Robin moaned. "Come here."

He didn't move. "The fuck are you doing?"

Robin announced forcefully, "Come here, now."

She reached for his hand and guided it to her breast—coated in slick, warm filth.

"Lick it," she whispered.

"No!"

"I said lick my tits, Gay Boy."

He hesitated.

Then obeyed.

The taste was awful.

Rot and ammonia and salt.

But her skin underneath was soft, sweet.

She lifted her top and bra completely off and threw it 5 yards away in a heap. She looked back at Nick, eyes wild. She smirked. She wiped her hands across her heaving breasts, leaving a filthy residue across both tits and her perfect nipples.

"Suck my tits, Gay Boy."

She grabbed the back of his head and rammed it into her. He sucked one nipple, then the other, gagging between licks. He couldn't believe how disgusting and hot this was at the same time. He hated the taste, the texture, but he loved how wrong it was. Something in the air had filled his head whispering lies into his brain. He must fuck her. Now. It has to be disgusting. Demeaning. It has to happen now.

She had his cock out already. Robin grabbed it without ceremony and smeared shit down the shaft.

He groaned as her coated hands slathered it back and forth. Back and forth.

"This is so fucked," he said.

She kissed him, biting his lip. "Then fuck me."

"But... diseases."

"Shut the fuck up!" She roared. She forced his head down with her filthy hands. He was on his knees. He pulled her shorts off. She turned, got on all fours, and smeared guano along her inner thighs.

He mounted her.

His cock slid into her in one smooth thrust—too easy, too hot.

They fucked like animals.

He grabbed her dreadlocks again. Pulled. Not hard—**not like before**. But enough to feel control.

Robin moaned, face against the shit stained stone.

Their bodies slapped together. Filth spread across their skin. Their legs left streaks on the ground. Guano stuck to their faces, their backs, their necks.

Robin came first—loud, choking, shaking.

Then Nick, grunting into her shoulder, cumming harder than he had since the forest began breaking them.

They collapsed together.

Breathing hard.

Covered in shit.

Literally.

Robin stared at the cave ceiling.

"Oh my God," she said.

Nick wiped his face. The back of his hand was black.

They both looked at each other.

Then laughed.

Then gagged.

"This is disgusting," Robin said.

"We're disgusting," Nick agreed.

She pulled away, curling into herself. "We need water. A fire. A fucking exorcism."

He lay on his back, dick soft, face blank. "We need out of this fucking forest."

Silence.

Then Robin whispered something in Cherokee.

Nick turned to her. "What did you say?"
She didn't answer.
The raven landed outside the cave mouth.
Watching. Always watching.

CHAPTER 19
The Lake

After they recovered from their disgusting sex session and hoped that the giant had gotten bored and left, they tiptoed out of the cave. They went down the mountain towards a valley to find some water to clean off in. They were pretty annoyed at themselves now. After the feeling and excitement of all of this crazy new sex wears off, they are just a couple of unbathed, sweaty, shit stained hikers. Reality sets in after the whispers stop. They are in grave danger, and they keep having sex. It's ridiculous. Plus, after the last new adventure with the guano, this is just gross as fuck, they both thought.

"We need a fucking bath, now." Robin said.

Sticky, raw, sore in ways they couldn't name. Guano caked behind their knees, dried on their necks, smeared across their hips. Robin's legs trembled with every step. Nick's chest was tight, his cock somehow both satisfied and ashamed.

Then they saw it.

A **lake**.

Wide. Still. Framed by sharp rocks and leaning trees. It shouldn't have been there—not this high in the Smokies, not near this cave, not on any map they'd seen—but there it was. The water reflected the sky with too much clarity. No ripples. No wind. Just glass.

Robin stopped and stared, breath catching. "That's... perfect."

Nick dropped his pack, already peeling off his shirt. "No arguments."

They moved to the edge like pilgrims to a shrine.

Robin stripped slowly, her fingers trembling on the waistband of her shorts. Her skin was still streaked with dirt and dried bat shit. She pulled off her tank top, revealing the smudged curves of her breasts, still faintly streaked with filth.

Nick dropped his pants in a heap, stepping free.

Neither of them looked away.

They walked into the water, side by side.

The cold hit like salvation.

Robin gasped. "Fuck, that's freezing—"

"Get it over with!" Nick dove under.

When he came up, sputtering, slick and clean, he let out a laugh. A real one. A sound that hadn't come from his chest since before the woods had started stripping them down.

Robin followed him under. Her dreadlocks fanned behind her like seaweed. When she surfaced, she was smiling too.

"Holy shit," she said, wiping her face. "I forgot what clean feels like."

"We are not there yet, babe."

They swam out a little farther, just past the reach of the rocks. They vigorously cleaned themselves the best that they could. Then after they were satisfied, they relaxed.

Then they floated.

Silent.

Their clothes drifted near the edge, soaking on the stones.

The only sound was their breathing.

Until Robin turned toward him and whispered, "I'm still horny."

Nick whipped his head around and gave her a serious glance. He didn't answer.

He didn't have to. He was too.

He swam to her, wrapped his arms around her waist, and kissed her.

It was gentle at first.

Then desperate.

Their bodies pressed together. Legs wrapped. Water lapped against their backs. His hands slid down to cup her ass. Her tits pressed into his chest. He kissed her neck, her collarbone, then pulled back to look at her.

Her eyes were wide.

Then they widened more.

She gasped.

"Nick—don't move."

"What—"

Something touched his leg.

Long.

Slick.

Alive.

Robin's hand shot to his arm.

Another shape slithered between them, wrapping around her thigh.

They both looked down.

Eels.

At least half a dozen.

Jet black. As thick as a wrist. They rose from the depths in slow coils, curling around arms and legs. One wrapped around Nick's calf, then his waist. Another looped under Robin's breast, lifting it like an offering.

Nick froze. "What the fuck—"

Robin's voice was sharp. "There are no eels in the Smoky Mountains."

"What? Are you sure?"

"There are no fucking eels here. Not this high. Not in freshwater. This isn't—" She gasped again as one coiled around her thigh and slid up. "This isn't right."

They should've swam to the shore.

Should've screamed.

But instead—

They kissed again.

Harder.

The eels didn't squeeze.

They caressed.

One wound around Nick's chest like a harness, slick against his nipples. Another looped around his thigh and brushed his inner leg—so close to his cock it twitched in anticipation.

Robin arched in the water, floating as the eels twined around her belly, her hips, one sliding between her breasts and lifting her nipple to Nick's mouth.

He took it.

Sucked.

Robin moaned.

"Fuck—oh my god—"

Nick's hands found her ass beneath the surface. The eels helped, holding her steady as he pressed into her.

They nudged him in.

They gasped together.

The water was their bed.

The eels their ropes.

Robin's voice was shaky but clear. "This is… this is so fucking weird."

Nick nodded, thrusting slow. "I know."

She looked down at one eel pulsing around her thigh. "They're helping us."

"Feels good."

"Too good."

"I don't care anymore."

Another eel brushed against her clit as Nick thrust into her.

She screamed. Loud. Wet.

"Holy fuck—"

Nick kept going, harder now, wrapping one hand in her hair. An eel slid between his ass crack. He liked it. Another slid between hers. It was like extra hands, almost an orgy.

Robin clutched his shoulders, nails digging into his skin.

The lake rippled now. Only where they were. The rest of it stayed still—**unnaturally still.**

Birds didn't sing.

Wind didn't blow.

Only the moans.

Only the sound of water churning.

And their bodies.

Slap.

Slap.

Slap.

The eels' movements intensified, keeping time with the love-making: writhing with them like some underwater chorus.

Robin was close.

She could barely breathe.

Every time she tried to focus on what was happening, an eel stroked something else—her back, her ass, her clit, her neck, her asshole. It was rapturous.

Nick sucked her nipple underwater.

He kissed her throat.

He bit her shoulder and didn't say sorry.

When they came, it was together—violent, gasping, choking with pleasure and confusion.

Robin's head rolled back. Nick cried out against her neck.

They clung to each other like the water would steal them.

After a short time, the eels unwound.

And vanished beneath the surface.

The couple swam back to shore in silence.

Waded out.

Collapsed naked on the mossy bank.

Robin looked up at the sky.

Nick stared at the water.

Neither spoke for a long time.

Then Robin whispered, "That wasn't real."

Nick didn't answer.

She turned to him. "Was it?"

He shook his head. "It felt fucking real to me! We are freaks, Robin. Freaks!!" he laughed.

She nodded slowly.

Then: "I loved it."

Nick looked at her.

"So did I. A lot. When we get back home... let's buy an eel."

CHAPTER 20
The Liver, I Eat It.

She did not walk.

She levitated.

Through the branches, through air heavy with rot and memory, through folds in the forest that only she could find. Spearfinger did not leave prints. She left silence.

She was the hunger of the mountain.

The black blade of its fingernail.

And she watched.

The lake first.

Robin and Nick floated near the center, limbs entangled, skin glistening in the dying light.

From her perch above, Spearfinger saw everything. No breath. No blink.

They were slick with desire and confusion. They kissed like addicts—needing and hating it all at once. The eels had wrapped them in wet coils, their bodies guided by the forest's will. One slithered between Robin's thighs as Nick entered her again. Robin threw her head back, moaning against the windless air.

They climaxed together, water erupting around them like they'd stirred the lake's heart.

Spearfinger tilted her head.

She wanted to wear Robin again.

She wanted to know what it felt like to drown while moaning.

But not yet.

She turned.
The trees parted.
The forest shifted.

Butch.

He was in a clearing, shirtless, legs braced wide. His muscles glistened, his hands firm and wide as dinner plates.

The woman in his grip was small. A forest ranger—tan uniform shirt bunched under her arms, face flushed. Her bright red ponytail whipped behind her as he lifted her **straight up**—arms fully extended above his head—her back arched, thighs splayed.

Her cunt pressed directly against his mouth as she was lifted into the air like a ballet tandem.

She shrieked.

He **devoured her**—grunting between wet licks, locking his arms beneath her knees, turning in slow circles like a bear showing off its kill. Spinning in 360 degree circles, she never felt anything like this before as her thighs rested on his broad shoulders, his hands holding her up by pushing her back into his head.

Her hips bucked. She moaned, trying to grind deeper onto his face.

And Butch kept spinning.

When he dropped her, she gasped, her legs shaking, knees unable to hold.

He caught her mid-fall and slammed her against a tree trunk, lifting her again by her ass, burying his cock inside her with a single, brutal thrust.

"Fuck me," she begged. "God, **fuck me**."

He pounded into her, the tree shaking behind them. Leaves shook off the tree. Animals scurried away from their elevated homes in fear.

And Spearfinger saw it.

The fracture.

The thing behind Butch's eyes. The broken place.

He wasn't trying to fuck her.

He was trying to **kill something inside himself.**

And the little red-headed forest ranger knew something like that was going on, but she didn't care. She was being fucked by this strange mountain of a man who was satisfying her needs better than her sweet, doughy husband ever could.

She moved again.

Back into the thick.

Back into the whisper.

Trevor.

Sitting on a mossy rock, pants bunched around his knees, flashlight propped in the crook of his arm.

He stared at a single **Polaroid**—bent, stained, nearly torn, well-loved.

Robin, naked. Nick buried in her. Her back arched. His hand in her hair.

Trevor stroked him self slowly, eyes glossy. His breath hitched with guilt.

"Fucking hell…" he muttered, "Her fucking tits... MMMMMMM...".

He came with a hiss, shivering, biting down on his knuckles.

Spearfinger stood behind him.

Ten feet.

Unseen.

"

Her long finger flexed once.

She could have pierced him then.

But she wanted him to **fear it first**. She likes to play with her food before devouring it.

She turned once more.

The forest went still.

No birds. No rustling. Even the insects tucked themselves beneath bark and stone.

She arrived at her place.

The place the Cherokee had once whispered about but never found.

A low hill, crowned with black stones arranged like teeth. Roots curled from the ground like veins. The moss glowed faint green, even in darkness.

She stepped into the circle.

The raven came down from the trees and landed on a boulder beside her. It clicked once.

Spearfinger sang.

Low. Crooked. Slow.

The melody had no real words—just sounds of mourning and hunger, carried from throat to earth.

She held out her long obsidian finger and carved a slow spiral into the dirt.

A symbol for **hunger**.

A symbol for **home**.

The raven clicked again.
She whispered, "The liver…"
Stroked its head.
"The liver…"
The bird turned one eye to her.
"I eat it."
The spiral pulsed.
Something far below the ground **listened.**
And the trees began to lean in.

CHAPTER 21
The Reek of Fire

They sat naked in the dirt, steam still rising off their skin.

Robin's legs were tucked under her, her bare thighs streaked with droplets that clung like dew on satin. Her dreadlocks, wet and tangled, hung in thick ropes over her shoulders, beads and bits of forest debris threaded through them like accidental jewelry. Her back was curved like a sculpture, the muscles beneath her smooth bronze skin catching the firelight. Her full breasts, still glistening, rose and fell slowly, nipples dark and tight in the chill of evening.

Nick crouched across from her, his knees bent, elbows resting on them, staring at the small mess of twigs and bark he was arranging in a pile like it was a ritual. His chest was broad, with scratches across one pec and a bruise forming under his left nipple. His cock hung soft and wet between his legs, streaked with the drying remains of their earlier passion. He was too tired to be aroused again—but not too tired to want her near.

Their clothes were draped over a log near the lake, still dripping, heavy and limp like discarded skin.

Neither of them wanted to put them back on yet.

Too wet. Too cold. Too filthy.

Or maybe they just couldn't bring themselves to cover the skin that had finally felt somewhat clean again.

The forest was still.

Almost polite.

Robin tilted her head, watching Nick work. Her lips were swollen from kissing. Her thighs still ached from being wrapped around him, from grinding down on him in the water until they both cried out into the fog.

She stretched, slow and unashamed, every inch of her body responding like a cat in sunlight. Her breasts lifted, round and weighty, the curve of her hips catching the last of the light. A trail of lake water ran from her navel down through the patch of curls between her legs, glinting like a silver snake.

"Try it now," Robin said, voice low.

Nick struck a match and held it low. The flame danced, then hissed out.

He growled. "Shit."

Robin stood and padded into the underbrush, moving like a dream. Her bare ass jiggled with each step, firm and full, and Nick couldn't help but stare. It was obscene how good she looked—even in this chaos, even surrounded by rot and death and dread. She returned with dried moss and dead leaves in her hand and set them in his palm without a word.

"Use this."

The next match caught.

The flame bloomed with a hungry crackle, licking at the moss and curling the leaves into blackened spirals. Within minutes, a small, fierce blaze shivered at the base of a crooked tree. The light danced across Robin's thighs, making them look like they were made of copper and fire.

Nick leaned back, palms flat on the earth. "God damn."

Robin knelt beside him. "It's beautiful."

They both stared into it, hypnotized.

Then the smell hit them.

Not smoke.

Not wood.

Something worse.

Thick. Chemical. Like old hair burning.

Nick sniffed. "The fuck is that?"

Robin leaned closer.

The fire twisted.

A strange green tinge licked the edges of the flame. It smelled like melting rubber and raw meat. It should have been unbearable—but they couldn't pull away.

Then the smoke rose.

And it changed.

Not just steam or vapor.

Images.

At first, it was just shapes. Twisting patterns. Shadows in motion.

Then a hand.

A pale hand reaching into the dark.

Then a finger—long and black and sharp—moving in slow arcs like it was carving the air.

Robin's breath caught. "Do you see that?"

Nick nodded, barely moving. "Yeah."

They leaned in.

The fire popped once—louder than it should have—and the image shifted.

Now a towel.

A white towel, soaked in something dark.

A man holding it.

Charlie.

He stood in a clearing, towel stretched between his hands, mouth open in song—but there was no sound. His eyes were wrong. Blank. His face didn't move when he sang.

Then—

His neck snapped sideways.

The smoke blurred.

Another scene rose.

A forest ranger, short and freckled, being lifted in the air.

Butch's face, mouth locked between her legs, arms flexed.

He spun her like a trophy.

Robin's voice was a whisper: "That's that giant who was watching us."

Another pop from the fire.

The smoke curled again.

This time: Trevor.

Sitting alone.

Masturbating.

Staring at a Polaroid. Her Polaroid.

Robin turned her face away.

Nick's fists clenched.

Then—

The image changed again.

Now it was them.

Robin and Nick.

Fucking.

On the ground. In the cave. In the lake.

Over and over.

Like a loop.

But the faces twisted.

Nick's eyes turned all white.

Robin's mouth opened too wide, jaw unhinged.

Then her face became Spearfinger's.

The fire cracked, and the image vanished.

Robin jumped up. "That's enough TV time for me, Nick."

Nick stared into the flames like he couldn't look away.

She grabbed a branch and knocked the pile apart, scattering the logs.

Smoke burst up in a hiss.

And was gone.

Just fire again.

Just heat.

Robin stood there breathing hard, arms crossed. Her bare chest rising and falling like she'd run a mile. Her nipples were still hard, and Nick watched her, transfixed. Not with lust. With awe. Like she was the last beautiful thing in a world gone mad.

Nick looked up at her slowly. "You saw all that?"

She nodded.

"I think it was... real."

Robin crouched down beside him again, knees wide, the damp between her legs catching the firelight. "It was watching us. The fire."

"Or showing us."

"Or both."

She leaned her head on his shoulder.

They sat again in silence.

Eventually, Robin pulled their shirts from the log and draped them near the embers.

Steam rose from the sleeves.

"Do you ever wonder," she said softly, "if this is hell?"

Nick didn't answer.

She kept talking. "Like we died on day one, and this is just the punishment? The test?"

Nick looked at her, finally.

She looked tired.

Beautiful. Bruised. Hollow.

He nodded. "Yeah. Every day."

She touched his cheek, slow and deliberate. Then leaned in and kissed him. A gentle kiss at first. But it deepened. Grew desperate.

They lay back in the dirt.

Robin straddled him, lowering herself onto his half-hard cock until he groaned beneath her. Her body moved slow and strong, muscles rippling in her legs as she rode him, her hands on his chest for balance.

Nick gripped her thighs, then her waist, then let his fingers glide up her back. She was warm again. Slick again. Alive.

Their rhythm built like a storm—her ass slapping down onto his hips, breasts bouncing, her eyes wide and locked on his. She whispered his name, over and over, like a prayer or a spell.

He came inside her with a grunt, arching up into her, feeling the firelight burning across his face.

Robin didn't stop.

She leaned back, riding out the tremors, one hand between her legs, moaning into the darkness.

When she finally collapsed onto his chest, both of them were covered in sweat and dirt again.

But it felt right. It was sweet. It felt like "them" making love- old school Robin and Nick- not the woods controlling them.

The filth. The fire. The way their bodies wouldn't quit each other even when their minds screamed for peace.

They held each other.

They didn't see the raven perched in the tree above them.

Didn't hear the branch creak.

Didn't feel Spearfinger's gaze through the flames.

But she was there.

And the smoke still curled, faint and dark, in the shape of a spiral.

CHAPTER 22
The Camera Returns

The fire was nothing but red coals now. The sun had dipped low behind the trees, spilling a soft bruised gray across the sky like a healing wound. A breeze stirred the steam from their clothes, which still hung in stiff, half-dried folds on a log by the fire.

Robin sat cross-legged in the dirt, naked except for a towel over her shoulders. Her legs were goose-pimpled. Her dreadlocks clung to her skin like roots to stone. The last of the day's warmth seeped from her bones, but she didn't move. Her arms hugged her knees. Her eyes were hollowed out.

Across the fire pit, Nick paced barefoot along the lake's edge, kicking pebbles into the shallows. He kept running his hand through his hair, over and over, like he was trying to dig something out of his skull. Every now and then he'd pause, stare at the treeline, then shake his head and keep moving.

He hadn't spoken in ten minutes.

Robin reached for her pack.

It felt heavier than it had earlier.

That was strange. She frowned, unbuckled the top flap, and paused.

Inside, buried under some crumpled clothes and a crumbling roll of toilet paper, was a dirty towel. She didn't remember putting it there. She didn't remember any towel at all.

And wrapped inside it—

The Polaroid camera.

She froze.

Her breath stalled in her chest like it had forgotten how to move.

The camera lay nestled in grime, its edges crusted with old dirt, maybe blood. Definitely blood.

Her fingers trembled as she lifted it out.

The weight of it pulled at her wrist. Heavy. Solid. Too real. As if it had mass beyond physics. As if it held something more than plastic and mechanics. Something deeper. Older.

She ran her fingers along the cold surface. A tiny part of her hoped it wouldn't work anymore.

She pressed the shutter.

Whrrrr-click.

The camera whined to life like it had just woken from a dream. A photograph began to push from the slot.

But this wasn't new.

It had already developed.

Already waiting.

Robin's stomach tightened.

She didn't move.

"Nick," she called.

He turned, arms frozen mid-swing. "What?"

She held up the camera.

He saw it, and his face went pale. That warmth he carried from the day's last touch of sunlight drained right out of him. "Where did you get that?"

"In my pack."

"We… we left it in the ranger station."

Nick took a slow step forward.

Robin was already spreading the towel out across the dirt, making a kind of work surface, her hands working automatically. The camera sat in the center, fat and silent.

She reached behind it.

Slid out the photo.

Another one followed.

Then another.

They counted nine photos.

She laid them out carefully, one by one, like tarot cards.

The first: **Charlie**, holding a towel like a banner, mid-song. His eyes were wide. His neck was wrong, bent at an impossible angle.

Robin covered her mouth. "Jesus."

The second: **The ranger**, pinned to a tree. Butch stood behind her like a beast, teeth bared, wild-eyed, mid-thrust. Her mouth open—in rapture.

The third: a **blur of motion**, dark in the woods. Branches or limbs—too many of them. No clear shape. It looked like a tree… or something pretending to be one.

The fourth: **Trevor**, sitting on a rock, pants down, a Polaroid in hand. The angle was behind him. High. Like a Hollywood jib shot or taken from somewhere high up in a tree.

He was staring at the fifth photo: a close-up of Robin's face, her mouth open in a silent scream. Her eyes were full of tears. A black hand—long-fingered, obsidian—brushed her cheek with a grotesque tenderness.

The sixth: **Nick**, asleep, curled on his side. His face had no features. Just smooth, blank skin where his eyes, nose, and mouth should've been. He looked like a sculpture of himself made by someone who had only heard vague rumors of what a human was. There were vine tendrils reaching out, wrapping around his wrists and ankles.

Nick recoiled. "No."

Robin reached toward it. "Let me see—"

"I said no." He snatched it up and turned it over. The back was blank. No timestamp. No handwriting.

No clue.

The seventh: **the lake**, shot from the shore. The surface still, glassy. But under the waterline—just barely visible—were dozens of pale faces. All pressed to the underside like they were trying to surface. All smiling.

Robin swallowed hard.

The eighth: **her**, sitting alone in the dirt. The trees were gone. The sky behind her was pure black—no stars, no moon, no clouds. Just void. Yet she smiled. Like it was peace. Like she had accepted something terrible.

The ninth: an overhead shot. A wide view from high above the forest. A ring of five bodies surrounded a dying fire, their arms stretched outward like spokes. Heads pointed away from the flame.

Nick counted. "One... two... three... four... five..."

"Us?" Robin asked.

"I don't know. Its... too high up. Too blurry."

They stared at the photographs.

The fire popped.

A pinecone hissed in the coals.

But the woods—utterly still. Even the birds were silent. Even the wind had ceased.

It was like the trees were listening.

Robin's voice came soft. "It's not just taking pictures."

Nick nodded. His throat worked to find words.

"It's showing us things. Things that haven't happened. Or that…" She trailed off.

"Maybe someone is just trying scare us with an A.I. trick."

"Or maybe its things that *will* happen. Or maybe things she wants to happen."

Robin picked up the photo of herself smiling in the void. "I know that is not me," she whispered.

But it was.

She knew it in her soul.

And so did Nick.

She gathered the photos into a small canvas pouch, hands moving slow, like she didn't trust herself. She didn't want them. But she couldn't destroy them. That felt… worse.

When she reached for the one of Nick faceless, he looked away.

"I hate this," he said.

"I know."

She slipped it in with the rest and tied the pouch tight.

They sat in silence.

Long.

Heavy.

She looked at the lake.

She thought about the faces just under the surface, smiling. Waiting.

She thought about the black hand stroking her face. The void behind her smile.

What if these weren't warnings?

What if they were instructions?

What if they were… invitations?

A chill ran through her belly.

The forest around them felt charged again. Like something massive and ancient had just finished listening. And was now deciding what to do.

The camera hadn't made a sound since they'd examined the photos.

But   then—

click.

All on its own.

No hand touched it.

No wind blew.

Just *click.*

Robin's head snapped toward it.

Nick stood, fast.

They stared at it.

The camera whirred again.

Another photo slid out, slow, like it was hesitating.

Robin's breath caught.

Nick stepped forward, but she grabbed his arm.

"Don't," she said.

He stopped.

The photo slid the rest of the way out.

Still developing.

The image slowly emerged—gray first, then contrast, then shapes.

A fire.

A body.

Blood.

Lots of blood.

Robin turned away.

Nick bent, trembling, and picked it up.

It was a picture of him.

Dead.

Naked.

Pinned to a tree with what looked like a spear through his chest.

And standing in the background—

Robin.

But not Robin.

Smiling.

CHAPTER 23
The Exchange

The trees opened into a clearing like a fresh wound.

Robin and Nick, freaked out already, were moving at a nice clip in a feeble attempt to escape the forest. They were now fully clothed. They turned a corner that lead to a clearing. They skidded to an abrupt halt. The three strangers were already there—Butch, Trevor, and Lane—standing still, backs half-lit by slats of sunlight. They weren't hiding. They weren't armed, at least not visibly. But they were waiting. Three black, very still, very scary, statues.

The groups stood in silence for what seemed like a full minute.

Butch stepped forward first. He looked even bigger up close. His eyes were bloodshot. He wasn't...right.

"We've seen you," he said.

"We've seen all of you," Trevor snickered, looking directly at Robin.

Robin and Nick didn't move. The silence between them all buzzed with something hot and fragile. Butch side-eyed Trevor. He didn't appreciate that kind of comment.

"We don't want trouble," Robin said carefully, hands half-raised, fingers splayed.

"Good," Butch replied. "Neither do we."

Trevor glanced at Lane. Lane's one good eye was locked on Robin. His blind white eye twitched faintly, as if sensing something hidden in her.

Nick shifted closer to her. "You been following us? Have you been killing these people in these Polaroids?"

Trevor ignored the insinuation, "You found something that wasn't yours."

Lane stepped forward. "The camera."

Nick's spine stiffened. "You're not taking it."

Lane stared, then tilted his head. "Why? Afraid of someone seeing the pictures you two have been taking?"

Robin swallowed. "We don't know who is taking these pictures. This is NOT our camera, It just keeps showing up. We were trying to find a forest ranger to—"

Butch opened one palm. "Let us see it. No violence. I give you my word. No one gets hurt tonight. But I really need you to hand it over, man."

Robin looked at Nick.

He didn't want to. Every muscle in him buzzed with refusal.

But she nodded. Slowly.

He unzipped the side pouch of his pack and handed the Polaroid camera over to Lane. Robin handed over the pouch full of Polaroids to a lustful Trevor.

Lane took the camera with both hands, reverent. His fingers ran along the lens, the flash. He didn't look up.

Nick clenched his fists. His brass knuckles were still in his pocket. Heavy. Cold. Itched to be used.

Lane handed the camera to the giant. Butch tucked it under his arm. "Go."

Nick blinked. "That's cute. It sounded like you, just now, were telling us to go."

"I said go. You don't want to be near us when we start looking at these pictures."

Robin didn't wait for clarification. She grabbed Nick's wrist and yanked him back toward the trees. "Nick!"

He let her lead, glancing over his shoulder just once.

They didn't chase.

Not yet.

***

They ran until their lungs burned, until the trees started to blur, until they nearly tripped over a fallen log.

Robin collapsed to her knees. "Fuck... fuck, Nick..."

He crouched beside her. "What's wrong? Are you okay?"

"No," she panted. "But we're out of there."

He looked back again. "I should have kicked their asses."

"No," she snapped. "No, you don't get it."

"What don't I get?"

"They saw me, Nick. They saw everything. They will see... ALL of me."

Her voice cracked.

"I should've smashed that camera into a tree. I should've thrown it into the river. Should have burned those pictures..."

"Baby, that's the least of our problems. And besides, those guys probably won't leave these woods alive."

She looked at him then. Really looked. "They were staring at me already..."

"Every red blooded American man does, Robin. And most of the women. You are a goddess. Come on, Queen. Let's go."

***

Back in the clearing, Butch set the camera on a flat rock.

They were starting to leaf through the Polaroids, but the camera made a noise.

It whirred.

Printed.

Without human interaction.

Trevor picked it up.

He chuckled.

Another.

Then another.

The three men leaned in.

Robin naked. Robin fucking. Robin bent over, riding Nick. Her face mid-orgasm. Reverse Cowgirl-mid shot- Robin's ass deliciously imploding on Nick's stomach.Lane didn't laugh. He just stared. Smiled.

Butch smirked. "Damn. She's so fucking hot. Why is she with a loser like that?"

As they looked through the pictures, Trevor slid a Polaroid into his cargo shorts. A shot of her riding Nick from the front, hair flying all over the place. Tits heaving, mid bounce, her lips mid-bite. Robin forcefully pressing into Nick's chest with both arms flexed.Butch raised an eyebrow. "She's not just a girl, though. You see her eyes? Something's living in there. She's fucked up."

Lane said nothing, but his lips parted like he was tasting the memory.

Robin mid-blowjob. Robin crying. Robin being ridden like an animal from behind.

"She's definitely not afraid of PDA," Trevor says. sliding that last Polaroid into another pocket."No," Butch said softly. "She looked… free."

The word hung in the air like a curse.

Lane leaned over the camera and hit the button again.

Another photo.

It developed slower.

This time, Robin stood alone. Naked. In the trees. Covered in ash or dirt or both. Her smile was wrong. Tilted. Off.

Trevor shivered.

"Man," he muttered. "Something's really wrong with this chick."

Lane pulled the next photo.

A blur. A hand. A mouth. A flash of Nick's face, distorted like he was screaming.

They didn't speak for a while.

Just stared.

Then the camera clicked again.

All on its own.

A new photo slid out.

Butch picked it up, slower this time.

It showed a man hanging from a tree.

Head tilted.

Neck stretched too far.

A giant.

Unrecognizable.

But wearing Butch's flannel.

Trevor took a step back.

"Nope. Fuck this."

Lane reached for his knife.

Butch held up a hand. "What do you think you're gonna do?"

His voice was calm. Hollow. Dead.

"We finish the photos."

Robin and Nick crouched behind a fallen tree miles away.Robin had her arms wrapped around herself. Nick kept watching her.

"Don't look at me like that," she said finally.

"Like what?"

"Like I'm possessed. Or broken. Or less than."

"I'm not."

"Yes, you are."

"I just want you safe."

Robin snorted. "That ship sailed the moment we stepped on this fucking trail."

She stood up and faced the woods.

"Let's get out. Let's find the road. Or a trail. Anything."They started walking.

But the path behind them... blinked.

Like an eye.

Like something watching. The forest was alive. Changing. They didn't notice the raven following them from branch to branch.

They didn't hear the whisper rise from the leaves: "She's already mine."

Butch stared at the camera longer than the others. His brows furrowed, then his eyes went wide. "This... this is Emma's camera," he muttered. "My daughter's! She brought it on her last trip. I remember this thing now. I can't believe I never noticed this before now!"

"How do you know it's her camera?" Trevor asked.

Butch tilted the camera's side towards his friends. Two letters dried on the silver metallic case in dark pink fingernail polish- E W.

CHAPTER 24
Proctor

Panic running, then trotting, eventually slow walking. They should've reached a trailhead hours ago.

But nothing looked right.

The forest looped on itself—paths reappearing in reverse, landmarks they could've sworn they passed already showing up again. The sun moved, but the shadows didn't seem to follow.

Robin hadn't said anything for a while. She has sobbed, several times now.

Nick huffed behind her, sweat darkening his shirt. His legs ached. The psychological and physical weight of the Polaroids he kept hidden from the strangers in his pack felt heavier with every step. These pictures were the most personal. The most sexual, the most macabre. At this moment, every breath tasted like rot in these cursed woods.

Suddenly, Robin stopped.

Nick nearly walked into her. "What's up?"

She turned her head slowly, her face blank.

Without a word, she took off her tank top. Her chest rose and fell with uneven breath. Her skin glistened in the humid light, every curve of her figure highlighted by the sweat and tension in the air. She was staring into the woods with a blank expression.

"Robin—"

But her eyes weren't quite her own.

"You ever get the feeling you're not alone in your own body?" she asked, voice soft but too calm. "Like something else is watching from the back seat." Her lips curled into a sly smile.

Nick frowned. "What are you talking about?"

Robin circled Nick and cupped her huge tits in her hands, fingers gently moving over her hard nipples. She didn't break eye contact, and had an impish smile the whole time. She circled Nick a few times and never broke eye contact. Eventually, her own caresses on her body started to take it's toll. Her smile dissipated, and she couldn't keep eye contact any longer. She half closed her eyes and started to moan. Nick, exhausted and not in the mood for this at all, felt his cock twitch.

"Here we go again with this crazy shit." Nick muttered, but as he lustfully looked at Robin contorting in front of him, something to the left caught his eye. His head darted in that direction. A group of furries... wait... the same group from the elevator, looking at him in the brush with animated approval. His dick got immediately hard.

Nick looked down at his cock, "The fuck?"

Robin was too busy playing with herself to notice. She sat down on the mossy ground, her breathing growing heavier. Her eyes fluttered shut as if she were listening to something only she could hear. She touched her chest—lightly, almost reverently.

She then spun, into a position where she was on all fours.

Her head started whirling in circles as she plunged two of her fingers into the soft folds of her delicious pussy. It was so wet already. "How can I be so horny and so afraid at the same time? Why am I doing this?" She thought. Her fingers slid in and out, but it wasn't her movements. Her hands were being controlled by someone, or something else.

She gradually became an animal in front of Nick with her increasingly violent masturbation. Beast like moans. Her head thrashing to and fro. She was experiencing the best masturbation session of her life. She came multiple times. Post orgasm number four, while her hips started to thrust against her own hands again, she looks up at Nick before the ride started going out of control again. Her eyes were black.

"Enjoying the show, gay boy?"

"W-what?"

"Why aren't you fucking me?"

"I- I don't know... I mean, this is crazy Robin. I feel like we are in imminent danger."

"Gay boy wants his furry friends more than his hot ass cum slut!" she moaned.

She looks at the clearing where Nick saw the furries in the brush. He thought it was a hallucination that he could only see.

Robin is riding her hand insanely hard at this point. The grass beneath her is becoming soaked with her juices. Thrusting up and down on herself at a machine's pace, Nick thought her violent motions resemble pistons in an engine.

"GO FUCK THEM!"

"GO FUCK THEM!"

"GO FUCK THEM!"

Inexplicably, Nick felt his dick twitch and the urge to walk over to his imaginary elevator companions. He stopped himself. One reason was shame, because he was surprised that he had half a thought to go fuck the furries in the woods... and to possibly be fucked.

"What the hell..." he thought. "What are these woods doing to me?"

The second reason was that Robin's masturbation session has become so violent that she is thrashing her head so erratically as she screams "GO FUCK THEM!" that she is hitting her head on the ground.

Thud.

Thud.

Thud.

By the third sickening thud, Nick races over to physically stop this insanity. He picks her up in a swoosh. Nick's muscular arms stop this thrashing quickly and gently. She was still shaking from the orgasms inside her loins. She was not quite back yet. Something else was still inside.

Then her hands paused. Her eyes opened again—this time sharp, focused on him.

"Robin! Robin!" he said, his strong hands controlling her arms.

Robin blinked and suddenly gasped, ripping away from his grasp and covering herself. "What the hell just happened? OW! My head! What did you do to me?"

"You zoned out," Nick said, crouching next to her. "Said some weird stuff. Like something was taking over. You started masturbating like a maniac and then you started banging your head into the ground."

She grabs her head. "It felt like I wasn't in control. Like a dream I couldn't wake up from."

Nick helped her up. They moved slower now, sticking close together as the woods changed around them. The trail narrowed. The air grew thick.

Robin's head was throbbing. But so was her insides. Whatever happened, was terrible. And she liked it.

Then the trees parted.

There it was.

Proctor.

The ghost town rose like a memory—only a few weathered cabins remained, splintered fences, and a church foundation. Vines clung to the few remaining buildings like the forest was trying to reclaim them.

Robin shivered. "Oh my God, this is the ghost town of Proctor!"

They walked cautiously into the town. A breeze stirred a string of bones hanging from a branch.

On the church door, pinned with a splinter of wood, was a Polaroid.

Robin pulled it down.

It was her.

Sitting nude on a broken pew in a church that was no longer there.

Smiling.

But her eyes were gone—replaced with two dark voids.

She clutched the photo to her chest, trembling. "I've never been here. But that's me."

Nick took her hand. "We need to keep moving."

Because the woods were still watching.

CHAPTER 25
The Polaroid Prophecy

The fire cracked low in the pit. Trevor poked at the embers with a stick, his jaw tight. Butch sat on a rock nearby, staring into the woods, fruitlessly watching for Emma. Lane crouched by the Polaroid camera, flipping through the images they've gathered so far.

Nobody spoke. The tension between them was thicker than the smoke from the fire.

Click.

The camera whirred and ejected a photo. Everyone looked at the magical contraption.

Lane caught it mid-air.

His brow furrowed.

"Another one," he muttered.

Trevor stood. "What is it?"

Lane flipped the image toward the firelight, then stopped breathing.

Butch stood too, his shadow long behind him. "Let me see."

Lane hesitated—just a beat—then passed the picture over.

Butch stared.

It was Lane.

Lying on his back on the forest floor.

A machete buried in his skull.

Blood pooled beneath him, seeping into moss. His white eye stared out at nothing. The other—gone.

Trevor gagged.

"Is this a threat?" he asked. "Or... a warning?"

Lane said nothing. He turned away, fist clenched around the Polaroid, and threw it into the fire.

Butch didn't stop him.

Click.

Another photo emerged.

Lane didn't reach for it.

Butch did.

He turned it toward the flames.

It was Emma.

Butch's eyes were on fire- full of rage.

She was curled up in a dark corner. Alone. Afraid. Her clothes torn, her face streaked with tears.

But she wasn't alone in the frame.

Robin stood above her.

Naked.

Smiling.

One hand cupping her right tit. The other outstretched, palm hovering over Emma's head like a puppeteer.

Butch's eyes widened.

Robin's face—was wrong.

Not just angry. Not cruel.

Inhuman.

Her features had shifted—slightly stretched. Lips too wide. Shadows under her eyes. Her teeth longer than they should've been. Slightly higher cheekbones.

Emma looked like she was trying not to scream.

Butch stared at the image like it might burn him.

Lane stepped forward. "That's not that slut. That's—"

"Spearfinger," Butch said softly.

Trevor looked away. "Fuck."

Click.

Another photo.

Butch caught it again.

This one showed Robin kneeling beside Emma, holding her chin. Emma's eyes were wide in terror. Robin's mouth was open in a twisted grin, her tongue extended like a snake, hovering inches from Emma's cheek.

Butch gritted his teeth.

"She's tormenting her."

Lane nodded. "Wearing that girl's face."

Click.

A fourth Polaroid dropped.

Butch snatched it before it hit the dirt.

Emma, lying in a bed of dead leaves. Her hands over her face. Robin crouched beside her—no longer smiling. Just staring.

In the background, the raven perched on a stump. Watching.

Butch's face turned red. His breathing quickened.

Lane held up his hands. "Don't."

Butch turned toward him. "You knew."

"What?"

"You knew what they were. That girl—Robin and her dork-ass boyfriend. You're working with them."

"Working with them? The fuck? That's bullshit. Where is this coming from?"

"Is it? How come you're always calm when these two assholes show up? How come you never panic?"

Trevor stepped between them. "Butch—"

Butch shoved him aside. Something in the forest was skewing Butch's perception of reality. And with a man Butch's size... that's terrifying. His anger irrationally grew.

He charged Lane with a roar, fists flying.

Lane ducked, rolled, and came up fast. He caught Butch in the stomach with a sharp elbow, then twisted and slammed him into the dirt with a jujitsu hip throw.

But Butch was strong.

He surged up, grabbed Lane by the waist, and lifted him—slamming him against a tree.

Lane gasped.

"Butch! What the fuck!" Trevor yelled.

Butch grabbed a rock, picked it up with both hands, and swung it down at Lane's head.

Lane rolled at the last second, the rock crashing against the ground. Butch didn't let go of it. He raised the mid-sized boulder for another smash.

Lane caught Butch's arm with both hands. He grabbed Butch's outside pinky, a move he learned from wrestling his older brothers as a kid,—and twisted- forcing him to drop the weapon. Almost no one, no matter how big they are, can resist the pain of a pinky being twisted.

They struggled. Kicked. Swore.

Trevor grabbed for Butch's shoulders, trying to pull him off—but Butch elbowed him hard in the chin, sending him sprawling.

Lane finally got leverage and flipped Butch onto his back with a judo throw that simultaneously sweeps the leg and pushes one's torso back.

He climbed over him, pinning him down.

"Stop! This isn't helping!"

Butch bucked hard—breaking the hold—and threw Lane off him.

Both men lay panting in the dirt.

Bloodied. Bruised.

Silent.

Trevor sat up, dazed. "Jesus Christ..."

Butch blinked slowly.

The rage still burned in his chest.

But something else had crept in.

Terror.

He knew he lost control. That he wasn't thinking straight. These guys are his friends. They are trying to help him look for his lost daughter. They are taking their annual paid vacations for this torturous trek of woodland Agatha Christie hour bullshit. How could he turn so quickly?

"I'm... I'm sorry."

Click.

Another Polaroid dropped.

None of them moved.

Finally, Trevor crawled over and picked it up.

He looked at it—and froze.

Robin. Naked. Perfect. An hourglass.

She is in front of an old church foundation.

Her hand raised.

In the other hand—Emma's necklace.

The heart-shaped silver locket Butch had given her on her 16th birthday.

Butch stared.

His fists clenched.

"That's no mountain witch. She's just an evil evil cunt."

Lane sat up. "Dude, that's not that Robin chick. I know it. It is the witch. She's been speaking to me in the woods, wearing Robin's body. She is something we need to prepare for."

"Doesn't matter." Butch stood, wiping blood from his mouth. "They're together. I don't care if she's a real person or the devil herself. They're together, and that means Emma is alive... and close."

Trevor shook his head. "Or it means Spearfinger wants you to think that."

Butch turned. "Spearfinger. Fuck that. I'm done thinking."

Lane stood too. "We can't keep fighting each other."

"I know. Sorry."

The wind picked up.

Not strong—but strange. It didn't push from a direction. It spun around them. Twisting. Pulling. Whispering through the trees like distant chanting.

Trevor wrapped his arms around himself. "Feels like we're walking into the end of a horror movie where everyone dies.."

Lane didn't answer. He was checking his blade.

Butch stared ahead, unmoving. "We follow the photos."

Trevor hesitated. "And when we run out of pictures?"

Butch looked at him. "We end the movie our way."

Something cracked in the woods to the west.

All three turned at once—silent, ready.

But nothing moved.

Only the fire crackled.

The forest held its breath.

Then the sound of soft singing floated down from the canopy.

Not in English.

Not in Cherokee.

Just vowel sounds and minor keys. Melodic. Haunting.

"Is that… her?" Trevor asked, barely whispering.

Butch nodded. "She sings to the raven."

The three men stood together, backs to the fire, weapons in hand, eyes on the dark between the trees.

The song grew louder.

The chapter ended in silence—but not peace.

Only the sound of the raven circling above them.

And the woods, waiting to close in.

CHAPTER 26
The Fire Tower

The trees opened up just before sundown.

Nick spotted the tower first—a skeletal spire of rusted steel rising out of the forest like a middle finger to God. Five stories tall, it stood like the last tooth of a rotting jaw, its blackened staircase spiraling into the clouds.

Robin didn't pause. She broke into a sprint, thighs pumping, her bikini top clinging to sweat-slick skin. The scratches down her legs looked like tally marks.

Nick chased behind her, lungs burning. "Robin! What are you doing?"

She didn't turn.

Behind them, branches snapped.

"THERE!" Butch's voice bellowed from somewhere in the trees. Closer than expected. Closer than possible.

Trevor howled like a drunken dog. "You sick fucks! Where the fuck is Emma?"

Nick hit the first stair and bounded upward, steel groaning beneath his boots.

"Keep going!" he shouted.

Robin was already halfway up.

The tower swayed in the wind, moaning with every step. Rust flaked off the rails like scabs from a dying thing.

When they reached the top platform, the wind cut straight through them—howling from all directions. The door to the cabin was warped and swollen. Nick shoulder-checked it once, twice—

It burst open.

They tumbled inside.

The tower's cabin was smaller than it looked: a square box of mildew, shattered windows, and rot. The air was heavy with mold and old sweat. A rusted desk drooped in the corner. The mattress on the floor looked used. Recent. Gross.

Robin collapsed against the far wall, heaving, hair clinging to her cheeks.

Nick slammed the door shut and twisted the bent latch into place.

"Fuck," he breathed.

Then—

THUMP.

Boots on the stairs.

THUMP. THUMP. THUMP.

Like judgment day, climbing floor by floor.

What do they do?

Robin wiped her mouth with the back of her hand. Her lips were pale. Her eyes wide.

She turned toward the window—and the moment she caught her reflection, she froze.

Nick saw it too.

Robin stood perfectly still.

But her reflection smiled.

And blinked.

Robin didn't blink.

Her reflection did.

"Robin?" he asked. "Hey. Hey. You still with me?"

She turned. Something was off about the shape of her mouth. The way it stretched just a hair too wide.

Outside, the footsteps reached the top.

The doorknob rattled.

Nick yanked the brass knuckles from his pocket.

The door exploded inward.

Butch stood there—hulking, wild-eyed, blood already dried across one cheek. Behind him, Trevor held a machete in a trembling grip. And Lane hung at the back, watching with his one good eye.

"Where is she?" Butch snarled. "Where's Emma?!"

Nick raised his fists. "We don't know! Who the fuck is Emma!?! I've never seen her before in my fucking life you psychopath."

"Bullshit!" Trevor barked, jabbing the blade forward. "You've been out here fucking and filming! That Polaroid has been taking pictures of your bitch and his daughter. What- are you into some sort of sex club murder cult!?!"

"We haven't hurt anyone! Please! Stop!" Robin screamed.

Butch lunged. Nick swung. Brass met bone— Butch's head snapped sideways, but he didn't go down.

He growled and grabbed Nick by the neck, lifting him off the floor with brute strength and slamming him into the wall. The entire tower creaked.

Robin screamed. "Let him go!"

Trevor raised the machete and charged. Robin dove for a broken chair, swung it low, and caught him in the shin. He toppled, blade skittering across the floor.

Lane stepped in last.

He didn't scream.

Didn't attack.

Just stared at Robin.

"You're not you," he said calmly.

Robin looked up from where she crouched. "What?"

"She's in you," Lane said.

Something flickered across Robin's face. She stood slowly, as if remembering her own body for the first time.

Then—

CRASH.

A raven slammed into the glass, wings spread wide, feathers scattering across the floor. Old glass shattering everywhere. All players shielded their eyes from the projectiles.

The bird shrieked as it spiraled into the room, diving straight at Lane's face.

He flailed, stumbled back through the cabin door out unto the platform, caught his heel on the broken floorboard and fell back into the railing—

SNAP.

The old railing gave way.

"Lane!" Trevor shouted.

Too late.

Lane tumbled backward—arms pinwheeling—his good eye wide with disbelief. He plunged over the edge in a spin, the blind eye fixed to the sky.

Nick lunged for him, missed by inches.

Lane's scream was short.

The impact was shorter.

THUD.

Like a watermelon bursting on pavement.

Silence.

No wind. No birds. Just the tower swaying gently, like it was breathing.

Trevor backed away from the edge. "Oh fuck... oh shit... oh fuck."

Butch staggered back.

They all looked down through the shattered wood.

A body lay sprawled below, limbs twisted, the white eye staring at nothing.

Robin stood motionless.

Then she smiled.

Not her smile.

Not human.

"This is fucked," Butch whispered.

Nick nodded. "You think?"

Robin began to hum.

Low.

Slow.

A song like smoke over graves.

Polaroids began to flutter across the floor—dozens of them spilling from Robin's pack. Some curled in the corners. Others were damp. But all of them moved. As if caught in an unseen breeze.

Butch bent down to grab one—then froze.

It showed **Emma**.

Barely clothed.

Standing beside Robin.

Her stomach torn open. Her liver gone. Smiling.

Trevor stared at it. "What the fuck is this? What is this?!"

Robin's voice changed.

Lower. Hollow.

"The liver… I eat it."

Nick pulled Butch backward.

"Get the fuck away from her!"

Too late.

Robin's feet lifted off the floor.

Her toes pointed downward, arms spread wide.

Her head tilted back.

The humming grew louder. It echoed off the glass, vibrated in their teeth.

Trevor screamed and tried to run—but the door slammed shut on its own. The latch twisted. Locked.

Nick charged, tackled Butch as he lunged again.

The three men fell into a pile—fists flying, legs kicking.

Above them, Robin hovered.

Her eyes had gone black.

Dead.

Beyond dead.

The Polaroids on the floor began to burn at the edges.

One showed Trevor—impaled through the chest.

Another showed Nick—faceless.

A third showed Robin, drenched in blood, kneeling before the raven with her mouth full of something dark.

Outside, the sky boiled purple.

The wind howled.

And then—

BOOM.

Lightning hit the tower.

The walls rattled.

Support beams shrieked.

The cot flipped over. The desk collapsed.

The floor tilted an inch.

Then two.

A piece of ceiling gave way, crashing onto the floor beside them.

Robin's body pulsed mid-air with blue-white light, her hair floating around her like seaweed in water.

Trevor crawled to the door and screamed, "We have to jump!"

"To where?!" Butch roared. "We're fifty feet up!"

Nick stood, brass knuckles ready, and stared at Robin.

At whatever was left of her.

She looked down at him.

And smiled.

CHAPTER 27
The Fall and the Feral

The tower gave out all at once.

It didn't groan, didn't creak—it **screamed**. A sound like a train wrecking in the clouds. The fire tower sheared sideways, pulled by some invisible force, as if the air itself had grabbed it and said *no more*.

Metal shrieked. Bolts popped like bones in a meat grinder.

Trevor dove through the broken window.

Butch followed a half-second later, pushing off the frame with a grunt and grabbing a loose support cable. It snapped the moment he touched down, sending him tumbling.

Nick had one arm wrapped around a vertical beam when the wall tore free. The world flipped sideways, his stomach dropped, and he flew through the air. Not fell—**flew**. Lifted and discarded like a toy.

Above him, Robin hung midair.

Still glowing.

She didn't fall.

She didn't flinch.

She watched him spin through the air like a leaf in a blender. Her face didn't move. No fear. No panic.

Just calm.

Almost curious.

Then—

CRACK.

The fire tower hit the forest floor.

Wood exploded like shrapnel. Nails became bullets. Screws whizzed through the air like hornets.

The roof caved in on impact, folding in half like a rotted jaw snapping shut. Dust and ash rose like smoke, and for a second it looked like the tower was trying to stand back up—but it didn't. It slumped into the dirt like a body finally giving up.

Nick crashed into a slope of moss and broken stone, ribs-first. The wind shot out of him. His vision blacked. His shoulder screamed. He bounced twice, skidded, and stopped against a tree root, head spinning.

Nothing made sense.

Up was down.

Left was right.

He was bleeding from somewhere. Everything inside his chest felt loose.

"Nick!"

The voice sounded far away, but familiar.

Robin.

It sounded like her. Not the demon. Not the witch. Not Spearfinger.

Her.

He blinked through the haze. Shapes moved above him—blurry branches, dancing shadows, sky that had no business still being light. His lungs seized in short gasps.

Robin stood at the edge of the wreckage.

Barefoot. Pale. Her arms hung limp at her sides. Her skin was streaked with soot and scratches. Her lips trembled.

"Help me…" she whispered. "Please."

Her voice cracked.

It almost broke him.

But then—her eyes flickered.

Blue.

Then black.

Then blue again.

Then gone.

She stepped backward into the forest. Vanished.

Nick sat up slowly, gritting his teeth. His ribs screamed. His shirt was torn. Blood was trickling down his arm. His fingers didn't want to make a fist.

"Shit…"

Snap.

He turned—ready to fight.

But it was Trevor.

Limping. Blood running down the side of his face. One eye completely swollen shut.

"You…" Trevor gasped. "You're alive?"

Nick nodded. "Barely."

Butch emerged last, dragging one leg, shirtless, filthy. Blood streaked his beard. He still had his knife. His knuckles were raw and swollen.

"She didn't fall," Butch said.

"No," Nick answered. "She floated."

"That's not Robin anymore," Butch muttered. "That's… something else."

The wreckage behind them shifted.

Wood splintered again.

Then—**click.**

A camera shutter.

The unmistakable sound of a Polaroid.

A fresh photo fluttered through the air, drifting like a dead leaf, and landed at their feet.

Trevor picked it up.

His hands shook.

He flipped it over—and dropped it.

Nick picked it up.

The photo showed **Lane's body**—twisted, broken, crumpled like a doll dropped from a rooftop. And something crouched over it.

Robin.

Naked. Her face smeared with something dark.

Her mouth wide.

She was *eating*.

Her teeth were sunk into Lane's ribcage.

Blood ran down her chin like syrup.

Nick swallowed the bile rising in his throat.

Trevor turned and puked into the bushes. His whole body shook.

"She's gone," he choked.

"No. She's possessed," Nick said. "By this fucking thing called Spearfinger. It somehow got inside her. But Robin is still in there. I've just got to figure out how to save her. Whatever you fellas do, don't wear the jewelry you find in these woods and don't fuck Spearfinger."

Trevor piped up, "Wait, your girlfriend fucked Spearfinger? Did you see it? That would be hot as shit!"

Nick shot Trevor an angry glance.

Butch stared at the photo. His face was stone. "That… that was my friend."

They moved away from the wreckage together. Nothing forgives past transgressions and bonds men together like falling out of a crumbling fire tower does. No one knew where they were going. The sun had disappeared behind storm clouds, though there was no rain. The sky was just *wrong*—like something above them had died and was leaking shadow across the canopy.

They trudged for over an hour before they found shelter: a massive hollow tree, its trunk split like an open wound. The inside was dark, but dry.

They crawled in. Didn't speak for a while.

Butch insisted they rotate watch.

Trevor collapsed instantly, curled around his machete like it could protect him from dreams.

Nick sat at the entrance, brass knuckles clutched tight.

Butch knelt opposite, massaging his injured leg.

"What do you mean, its inside her?" Butch said suddenly.

Nick didn't answer.

"What if she wanted to be taken? Maybe she likes the power."

"What are you talking about? I think it had to do with this mojo necklace she found in the woods. She wore it around for a little while. Said it might be cursed or something. But she didn't just let it in."

Butch's eyes narrowed. "And then she fucked it. I dunno man. I think your hot ass girlfriend is a real problem. She just killed my friend."

Nick bristled. "What the fuck do you mean? You don't know her at all. Robin has never killed anyone!"

Butch leaned in. "I mean... what are you guys doing out here? Is she a whore? Are you that good in bed? Fucking in the woods non-stop. What is with you two? Are you in a sex cult? What are you two doing out here? How can you have sex this much when you both stink from hiking all day? If you aren't nymphomaniacs, then something is taking over your labito. Do you think that I could be onto something here?"

"I don't know."

"Your girlfriend? She's gone," Butch said coldly. "And you're next if you keep chasing her."

"Dude, that's my girlfriend. What am I supposed to do?"

"No, it's not. Not anymore."

That night, the forest did not sleep.

And neither did they.

Trevor snored, sure—but even in sleep, he twitched and muttered. Butch stared at nothing. Nick tried to close his eyes, but every time he did, he saw her.

Robin.

Naked.

Covered in blood.

Floating above him, whispering things in a voice not her own.

He finally drifted off just before dawn.

And dreamed.

Of a field of dead crows. Feathers soaked in bile.

Of a cave with a river of black water.

165

Of Robin—kneeling beside a fire—rubbing something slick and red across her nipples. Laughing. Saying, "You were always weak, Nick. She likes the strong ones."

He woke with his mouth open and a scream trapped inside.

Outside the hollow tree, the raven watched them.

Perched just a few feet away.

It cocked its head.

And somehow smiled.

CHAPTER 28
Blood in the Bark

The next morning wasn't morning.

Not really.

There was no sunrise. Just a dull gray seep that replaced the black. No birds chirped. No squirrels chattered. No wind. Just the crackling creak of trees adjusting their bones.

Nick was the first to move.

He crawled out of the hollow, groaning, one hand still wrapped around the brass knuckles like a toddler clutching a stuffed bear. His ribs still ached. His shoulder was worse. But the pain felt secondary now—like background noise in a nightmare he couldn't wake from.

The raven was gone.

But its feathers were everywhere.

A full dozen scattered in the grass. All black, all slick with dew, and one of them... had teeth on it.

Tiny. Human. Baby teeth.

Molars, rooted and bloody, braided into the feather's spine like trophies.

Nick backed away. He stumbled and clutched a nearby root for balance.

Behind him, Trevor stirred, whimpering in his sleep.

"Don't... don't show her... don't..."

Butch woke with a gasp. Eyes open. Knife already in hand. He scanned the clearing.

They gathered their supplies without a word. No one mentioned Lane. No one said Robin's name. The silence between them was colder than the fog, like a pact they'd all made in their sleep.

The forest didn't wait.

As soon as they moved, it moved with them.

Not behind.

Around.

The trees leaned in. The moss thickened. The light never changed, but time passed. Nick could feel it. A minute stretched for hours, or maybe they'd been walking for days.

The bones started small.

Bird. Squirrel. Rabbit.

Then a possum skull, freshly cracked.

Then a deer carcass, dried and hollow, liver gone.

Then a boot.

Still laced.

With a leg inside it.

Trevor dry-heaved. Butch bent down and touched the shin.

"Still kind of warm," he muttered.

Nick looked away.

The forest hummed now. Not loud. But always there. A low, droning vibration that tickled the bones of their skulls.

That's when they heard it.

The scream.

Not distant.

Not imagined.

Close.

A woman's voice. Torn with terror.

"Nick!"

Robin.

Alive.

Desperate.

It cut through him like a knife. He was on his feet in a blink, heart leaping, body moving before thought could catch up.

"That was her," he gasped.

Trevor grabbed his wrist. "No. No, man. That was *it.*"

"You don't know that."

"She's playing you, kid. Spearfinger, have you ever researched her? We have! This is what she does, she's like an American siren. Calling stupid sailors off of their boats- these poor dudes thinking that they are gonna get a little piece of ass, but instead, the sailors drown or get eaten by sharks. Don't be a stupid sailor, bro."

"I *know* her voice!"

Trevor didn't let go. "DO YOU? After the Polaroids? After what she did to Lane? To that deer? You think that's still Robin?"

Butch didn't say a word. Just watched.

Nick pulled free.

Stormed forward into the trees, following the voice.

Butch followed.

After a beat, Trevor cursed, spit, and followed too.

"Let's go drown together! Or maybe we get eaten by sharks. All because Momma has a hot ass."

The trees pulled back, reluctantly revealing a clearing.

And at its center was a tree.

No—not a tree.

A cathedral.

A monument.

A grotesque god carved from roots and bark and bones and shadow.

It was massive, taller than anything in the forest. Its bark blackened like burnt flesh. Its base split open like a mouth.

And tied to its trunk, naked and bloodied, was **Robin**.

She hung like a sacrifice. Vines wrapped around her wrists, ankles, throat. Her head slumped to the side. Her chest rose. Shallow. Painfully slow.

Alive.

Butch raised his knife.

Nick stepped in front of him.

"Don't. That's her."

"Or it's bait."

"I'm going to her."

"She's not yours anymore."

"She never was," Nick snapped.

Butch's face twisted, but he stepped back.

Nick walked into the clearing, each step heavy, air thick like oil.

Robin stirred.

Her head lifted. Her eyes opened.

Blue.

Tear-filled.

"Oh baby... help... me," she whispered.

He took her face in his hands. She flinched.

Her skin was warm. Real. Her breath smelled like blood and soil.

"I've got you, baby. I'm gonna get you out."

Behind him, Butch stepped forward, knife raised.

Robin's eyes flicked toward him.

"Nick…" she rasped. "Don't turn around."

He froze.

"What?"

"Don't."

Her voice trembled.

"She's behind you."

Butch paused.

Trevor screamed.

And then the air *ripped*.

A sound like silk soaked in bone broth—**sshhhhrrk**—followed by a choked gasp.

Butch's body jerked forward. A long, obsidian finger emerged from the center of his chest, slick with blood, twitching.

It slid back out—slowly.

Butch dropped to his knees, then face-first into the moss.

Dead.

His face, shocked with this expression: "How could it end this way?"

Robin screamed at the sight of the horror.

Nick turned, shaking.

And saw her.

Spearfinger.

She stood at the edge of the clearing.

Ten feet tall. Skin like cracked porcelain. Hair dripping down her back like river sludge. Her eyes were bottomless. Her mouth wide and red and full of too many teeth. Her right hand had four fingers, the fifth- a blade. A long, obsidian spear finger, curved and cruel.

She smiled.

"That was too easy," she purred.

Trevor bolted.

Disappeared into the trees.

Spearfinger didn't chase.

She stepped forward, hips swaying.

"I like the ones who fight. The ones who dream. The ones with shame…"

She looked at Nick like he was dinner. Like she knew his thoughts. His fears. His sins.

Robin shook against the vines.

"Don't let her in," she whispered.

Spearfinger laughed.

"Too late."

CHAPTER 29
Brass Knuckles vs. Obsidian Blade

She didn't walk.

She *glided*, feet not touching the ground, the moss beneath her withering in her wake. Her blade-hand traced slow spirals in the air, and wherever the tip passed, the light bent—warped—like the air itself was retreating from her.

Her hair floated behind her like black water. Her eyes were pits. Her skin pulsed faintly with veins of obsidian.

And her breasts—too perfect, too full—rose and fell like they were breathing independently. The sight of them was dizzying. Hypnotic. Like staring into a pair of moons orbiting a black hole.

Robin sobbed behind Nick.

Still bound to the massive, ancient tree. Still naked. Her blood had dried in thick streaks across her thighs, her stomach, her breasts. Her dreadlocks hung limp over her face like tangled ropes. But her eyes—her real eyes—watched Nick with animal fear.

"Please…" she whispered. "Fight her."

Spearfinger cocked her head at Robin, then looked back at Nick.

"She wants a hero," the creature said. "You've never been one."

She pointed her blade-hand at his chest.

"You let me in the first time you saw her naked. You remember that? Your third date, in the backseat of your mother's borrowed automobile. How white trash of you two. And that pathetic little moan you made before she even touched you."

Nick gritted his teeth.

"She's not you," he spat.

Spearfinger's mouth split into a grin so wide it looked like it would tear her face in half.

"Oh no?"

She dragged the obsidian blade down her own collarbone. No blood spilled. Instead, black mist poured from the wound—wrapping around her curves, painting her skin darker, redrawing her form.

Her hair twisted into dreadlocks.

Her thighs grew thick and strong.

Her breasts bounced, firm and round. Turned into familiar shapes.

Her hips widened. Her ass rose into a perfect sphere, just like his girlfriend's.

She became **Robin**.

But not quite.

The lips were too red. The eyes stayed black. Her voice, when it came, was Robin's tone—but wrong.

"I can be her," she whispered, taking a step toward him. "I can be better."

Nick stepped back.

The brass knuckles shook in his hand.

Spearfinger's Robin-form walked slowly. Her bare feet hovered an inch above the moss.

"I know what you want," she said. "You didn't come here to hike. You didn't come here for peace.

You came here to fuck. You came here to run from the man you are. The shame. The trophies. The nights you couldn't sleep because you were afraid of who you really wanted."

"What?"

"You came here hoping the woods would purify you," she said. "But they exposed you."

She was inches from him now.

"You're a fraud, Nick. You want to feel power. But not to wield it. You want to be taken. To be used."

He lunged.

Fist flying.

Brass knuckles met face—**CRACK**—and she didn't flinch. His knuckles split. Blood oozed between his fingers.

Spearfinger grinned wider.

She grabbed his wrist with her free hand and yanked him close, her forehead pressing to his.

Her breath was hot. Wet. It smelled like burned hair and rotting peaches.

"Flesh is truth," she said.

Then she *kissed* him.

Hard.

Her tongue slid down his throat. It was too long. It moved like it had joints.

Nick gagged.

He felt it. Something sliding into him. Something wriggling behind his ribs.

He shoved her back, fell to his knees, choking and spitting.

Spearfinger moaned softly.

Behind her, Robin screamed. "Nick!"

He looked up, eyes red, chest heaving.

And Spearfinger changed again.

Now she was **Emma**.

Butch's daughter.

Small. Bare. Crying.

Her voice came in Robin's cadence.

"Daddy… why'd you leave me?"

Nick turned away, trembling.

He pressed his forehead to the ground.

"This isn't real," he muttered. "None of this is real…"

The moss pulsed beneath his face.

It was breathing.

Robin struggled in the vines. "Don't let her trick you. Please, Nick, she's inside me. She's *wearing* me. But I'm still here. I'm still me. Please free me!"

Spearfinger grew tall again. Her full form. White and smooth and glistening. Her obsidian finger dragged slowly across her belly, leaving no wound—just lightless streaks.

"Come with me," she said, her voice now in a tone he hadn't heard before—low, maternal, almost tender. "Be reborn."

Then she whispered something else.

Not English.

Ancient.

The word curled in the air and entered his ears like a spider crawling into his brain.

His thoughts froze.

His arms drooped.

His eyes fluttered.

The forest bent around him.

He was back in Memphis.

At a dojo. He's a teenager again. Shirtless. Lean. Nervous.

The small crowd cheered around him.

He'd just lost the judo final.

Second place.

Silver medal.

A furry in a pink rabbit costume stood in the corner of the gym, beckoning.

Nick looked down.

He was naked.

Hard.

The gym floor turned into moss.

He blinked and the clearing returned.

His mouth was open.

His hands—trembling—reached toward her.

And then—

"Nick..."

Robin's voice. Soft. Human.

His eyes locked on her.

She was crying now. Real tears. Real fear.

"Don't let her in," she said again. "You're stronger than her. You know it."

Spearfinger bared her teeth. "He's mine now."

And then Nick did something strange.

He smiled.

Just slightly.

And drove his brass knuckles upward—into **his own nose**.

CRACK.

Blood gushed.

Pain surged like lightning through his skull.

The spell broke.

Spearfinger was... surprised.

Nick roared through the pain. "You can't have her, you bitch!"

He dove, wrapping both arms around her midsection trying to football tackle her to the ground. She didn't budge. Her skin burned like dry ice. She thrashed—spun—sliced.

The obsidian blade missed his face by inches.

Robin screamed again. "Nick!"

He tackled Spearfinger into the moss. They crashed to the dirt. She writhed underneath him— stronger than anything he'd ever fought.

Her body shifted again—Robin, then Emma, then his *mother*.

He looked away. Slammed the brass knuckles against her temple.

Over and over.

"You're not her. You're not her. YOU'RE NOT HER."

Spearfinger howled with laughter.

Something black exploded from her body, splattering the moss, sizzling like acid.

She shrieked and kicked Nick off her with impossible force.

He flew ten feet and crashed into the tree trunk.

Robin's eyes met his.

Then—

A noise in the woods.

Trevor.

He was crouched, watching. Pale. Shaking.

Spearfinger's head whipped toward him.

"I see you."

Trevor stood up.

Panicked.

Turned.

And *ran*.

Spearfinger stood.

She stepped over Nick's broken, wheezing body.

Towards Robin.

"Time to finish it, love," she said.

The vines slithered tighter.

Robin gasped.

And then—

An eagle soared into view.

It dove from a mountain across the valley.

Cawing.

Talons like razor blades.

It struck Spearfinger's face.

She screamed and slashed in retaliation.

The bird dodged.

Nick blinked twice. There's a knife shaped shard of glass laying 6 inches away from his reach. Where did that come from? No matter. Nick grabbed the glass from the dirt and held it like a dagger.

Stood.

Blood pouring from his face.

Spearfinger turned—and Nick tried to jam the shard into her side.

He missed her ribs but caught the palm of her hand.

Her eyes went wide.

She screamed.

The tree behind them shook.

Vines snapped.

Robin fell forward on all fours.

Spearfinger vanished.

He rushed over to her, she was sobbing.

"I'm here. I'm here."

She coughed.

"I… I think I'm me again."

Nick quickly turned his head back and forth as he held his love.

Spearfinger was still nowhere to be seen.

CHAPTER 30
Victory

Nick held her.

Robin trembled against him, her skin cold and damp.

He looked at her hands, her shoulders, her face, her back—checking for injuries and simultaneously looking for any sign that this was another Spearfinger trick. Was she really back?

But she was.

Her eyes were blue again.

Wet with tears.

"You came back," he whispered.

Robin nodded. "She let me go."

"Why?"

"I think… I think because you hurt her."

Nick glanced at the shard. At the smear of black across the blade. "It was her hand. I meant to hit her ribs. I missed."

Robin looked up.

"You hit her *palm?*"

"Yeah."

She shuddered. "Legend has it, that she holds her heart in her hand, and it was the only place she could be killed."

Nick stared at the shard.

He murmured, "The palm of her hand."

He wrapped the shard in a torn shirt and stuffed it back in his pack.

They were alone now. The clearing still smelled of blood and ash. But nothing moved. Even the trees seemed to lean away from the place where she vanished.

Lane was dead.

Butch was dead.

Trevor had vanished.

Emma—still missing.

Robin naked, shivering.

Nick broken, but alive.

They walked.

No plan.

Just away.

From the roots.

From the tree.

From the black place in the center of the woods.

They found a dry gully where the soil was soft enough to rest. Robin curled against him, barely breathing.

Her body was exhausted, but her mind was wide open.

"She never really left," Robin said quietly.

Nick didn't answer.

"She was still inside me when you held me. Watching."

"You're free now."

"I don't think anyone who's touched her is ever free."

She turned her hand palm-up.

"Maybe that's why her weakness is her palm. Maybe it's the only part of her that ever *held* anything. Loved anything."

Nick didn't like the poetry of it.

He just wanted this to be over.

They rested until dusk crept in again.

That's when they heard it.

A voice.

Far off.

Calling:

"Daddy...?"

Robin's body tensed.

"That's her," she whispered. "Emma."

Nick stood.

Robin struggled to her feet. Still trembling.

They followed the voice.

Through the trees.

Up a hill of red roots and moss.

Until they saw him.

Trevor.

Down in a hollow, crouched beside something in the dirt.

He turned when he saw them.

His eyes were wide. Red. Insane.

"She's here," he said. "I found her."

Robin stepped closer.

A shape lay in the brush.

Small.

Still.

But it wasn't Emma.

It was a *Polaroid.*

Fresh.

Still developing.

Nick picked it up.

It showed Trevor.

Dead.

Eyes open.

Throat cut.

Laying in this exact hollow.

Robin gasped.

Trevor looked down at his hands. At the blood on his shirt.

And began to scream.

CHAPTER 31
The Deep Recess

The sound of Trevor screaming echoed through the trees long after he vanished.

Robin and Nick stood at the edge of the hollow, staring down at the crumpled Polaroid still fluttering in the dirt. It showed Trevor—dead. Eyes open. Throat cut. The same hollow. The same dirt. A mirror of the present moment, frozen in a future not yet written.

Or maybe already written.

Robin crouched and picked it up.

"It's still wet," she whispered. "It just developed."

Nick didn't move. He watched the shadows where Trevor had run.

"That poor bastard is gone."

Robin stood. Her legs still wobbled. "He's scared."

"All of his friends are dead. I'm scared too."

Robin looked at him.

There was a long silence.

Then she said: "Let's not lie to each other anymore."

"What do you mean?"

She held up the Polaroid. "We're being hunted by something that remembers the future. Or sees the future. And we're pretending it's going to be okay."

Nick ran his hands through his matted hair. He looked like a man halfway between prayer and punching something.

"No, no... These pictures have been all wrong. One showed that guy with the white eye getting killed by a machete. He fell off of a fire tower. That one showed Trevor dead here, right here... and he just now ran away. He's safe. She's just trying to wear us down with mind games. I hurt her, Maybe she is just a weak ass bitch. All bark and no bite. We must be strong. We need to keep moving," he said. "We find a way out of the woods. Or we find help. Or—"

"No one's coming," Robin said.

Her voice was flat.

Not scared.

Just done.

She turned and started walking.

"She's dead. I killed her. And now that she is- "

"You didn't kill shit," Robin interrupted. "She probably let you win that fight to fuck with us some more."

That thought hurt.

They walked for hours.

The terrain changed beneath their feet—moss became dry leaves, then loose stone, then sand. Tree bark grew darker. Even the air changed. Cooler. Thicker. Like stepping underwater.

No trail. No signs. The sun dipped behind the trees, and the forest grew colder.

Robin stumbled once. Then again.

"Here," Nick said, offering his arm.

She hesitated—then took it.

They rested under a cluster of bent pine trees that looked like they'd been twisted by hand. Nick built a fire from twigs and dry bark. It hissed but caught.

Robin sat across from him, her knees pulled to her chest. The oversized shirt he'd given her was torn and soaked. Her legs were scratched and bruised. Her lips were cracked. She's wearing the black lacy panties Nick had found to hide her modesty and that's it. She's gonna freeze tonight.

"You still love me?" she asked.

The question came out of nowhere.

Nick looked up from the fire.

"What?"

She didn't repeat it.

Nick's jaw tensed. "Of course I do."

Robin stared into the flames.

"Even after what she made me do? What you saw? What I let happen?"

"You didn't let anything happen. She's been controlling you. Us. All of us."

"She used my body. You didn't stop her."

"You begged me not to."

Silence.

Then Robin said, "You still liked it."

Nick didn't answer.

Because she wasn't wrong.

Even as he hated himself for it—he had liked it. Something about the power, the possession, the taboo. The way her eyes went black and her voice deepened. It stirred something in him he didn't understand.

"I don't want to talk about this," he muttered.

Robin laughed once, bitter. "No shit."

He stood. "I'll find water."

"You won't."

"I'll look anyway."

He turned and disappeared into the trees.

He walked for what felt like an hour.

There was no water.

Just more trees.

And the forest had changed again, even though he was still close to their camp.

The ground sloped downward into a basin filled with blackened bark and twisted roots. Trees had grown sideways here, their trunks curving like the bones of giant beasts.

Moss wept down the branches like hair.

The air smelled sweet.

Sticky.

And the temperature dropped.

Nick paused, suddenly aware that he was alone. Not just physically.

Alone.

Like no one would ever find him again.

He stopped and listened, his nerves were shot.

The forest exhaled.

And that's when the fog rolled in.

It came from all sides—thick, low, gray like cotton. It touched his ankles and climbed up his legs, dampening his pants, curling around his waist.

He turned to head back.

And found he couldn't.

The trail—if there had ever been one—was gone.

Just fog.

And trees.

And a single sound behind him.

Footsteps.

Slow.

Deliberate.

He turned.

Nothing.

He kept walking.

Faster.

But the steps behind him kept pace.

"Robin?" his voice cracked.

No answer.

"Trevor?"

Silence.

The fog thickened.

His heart pounded.

Then—

A figure appeared through the mist.

Female.

Tall.

Nude.

Hair down her back like dark silk.

Hourglass figure.

She didn't speak.

She just stared.

Nick took a step forward.

"Robin?"

The figure stepped closer.

It wasn't Robin.

Her hips were too wide. Her skin shimmered in unnatural ways. Her eyes were bottomless.

It was her.

Spearfinger. The real Spearfinger.

But softer now. Less monstrous. She looked… beautiful.

The blackness in her eyes no longer threatened—it invited.

She smiled.

"I missed you," she said.

Nick stumbled backward. "Shut the fuck up, monster. I thought I killed you."

Spearfinger laughed a deep laugh. It was insane to hear her laugh like that. Like a person.

"And yet, sweet boy, here I am in all of my glory." She looked down at her body and opened her hands in an inviting posture. She looked down at her toes, her perfect thighs, full breasts with pointy nipples, and then slowly up into Nick's face to make eye contact with a smirk.

"You vanished," he said.

Spearfinger laughed. "Little boy, something like you doesn't get to kill something like me."

She moved toward him, slowly, her feet brushing the moss without sound.

"You've been pretending your whole life," she said. "Pretending Robin was enough. Pretending your dreams didn't matter. Pretending you didn't want this."

"Didn't want what?"

"Pretending you do not wish to lie with your own."

"Shut up."

"You think shame will save you?"

He turned to run—

And slammed into a tree.

Spearfinger was behind him now.

Her hand touched his back. Gentle.

Almost maternal.

"You want to know what it feels like," she whispered. "To let go."

"I don't want this, definitely not here in this Hell you created."

"Then why are you hard?"

He was shocked. He was. This conversation alone made him rock hard.

He gasped, humiliated, confused.

"You are controlling my body. You are tricking my mind. Just like you do with her."

She pressed her chest against his back. Her huge tits felt amazing against him. He could feel her hard nipples through his shirt."

"Oh, God. I can't do this. I'm not going to cheat on Robin with a murderous, cannibal witch," he thought.

"Let me show you something beautiful," she purred.

Her hand slid down his chest. Over his stomach. To his belt.

He tried to resist—but it was like his muscles had been turned to clay. His limbs heavy. His mind foggy. A deep pressure filled his head, like a hundred whispers all at once.

She turned him to face her.

Her body shimmered like wet stone under moonlight.

"You love her," she said, "but you'll always wonder what else there is."

"I don't want to wonder."

191

"Liar."

She pressed her lips to his, soft at first.

Then firm.

Then deep.

The world around them warped.

The trees bent in closer. The fog spun around them in a slow cyclone.

Her hands slipped under his waistband.

She pulled his pants down and stroked him, slow, deliberate.

Nick moaned—tried to stop himself, failed.

"No..."

They continued to kiss. It was rapturous. When he inhaled, she filled his lungs with her sweet breath. When she inhaled, he instinctively did the same. The entire time, alternating breath and heavy French kissing. They made out, hands traveling over each other's bodies, and he started to feel light headed.

"I can be anything," she whispered. "I can make you feel everything."

"OK," he said. But he was agreeing to anything now.

Her hand grew colder.

Slicker.

Her voice deepened, "Oh Nick... yes..."

And behind her, shapes began to move in the fog—faces—bodies—whispers rising like steam.

He was drowning in her.

And he let himself go.

CHAPTER 32
The Stone and the Shame

She stood naked before him.

Tall.

Curved.

Impossibly smooth.

Her body shimmered like wet obsidian in moonlight, every line of her perfectly defined. Her hips were wide and ancient, shaped like fertility idols carved in caves long ago. Her breasts were round, firm, and flawless, the dark nipples erect and beaded with dew that hadn't come from the trees.

She wasn't just beautiful.

She was built—a sculpture of lust itself.

Her legs were long, powerful, thighs just slightly parted.

Her stomach was flat, yet carried the softness of something that could hold life—or consume it.

Nick stared.

He didn't blink.

His breath caught in his chest.

Her face was nearly Robin's now—only… perfect. Too perfect. As if Robin had been carved into an icon, all flaws smoothed away, all human detail replaced with some fantasy version. Her lips were fuller, glossier. Skin glowing with impossible smoothness. Her eyes remained dark, pools without bottom.

And they watched him.

"I missed you," she whispered again.

Her voice echoed inside his chest like a second heartbeat.

Nick took a step back. His legs wobbled.

"Uh... Um..."

Her smile widened.

She stepped closer, hips swaying in exaggerated slow motion. Her bare feet barely touched the moss.

"Do you know what I saw in you the first time I laid my ancient eyes on you?" she whispered. "Hunger. A beautiful, terrible hunger that no woman has ever truly satisfied. Not Robin. Not your ex. Not the ones you never told anyone about."

Nick's voice cracked. "Robin... satisfies me..."

She smiled.

Her hands touched his chest.

They were cool—like stone that had lain in the shade all morning. Her fingers glided over his pecs, his ribs, his stomach.

He shivered.

"You're strong," she whispered, "but tired. So tired of pretending. Wouldn't it feel good… to stop?"

"I know you think I'm not real," she said. "I'm about to be the most real thing you've ever felt."

He shook his head. "You're a monster."

"I'm a mirror."

"No…"

"I'm what you don't say. What you don't ask for. What you wish someone else would force on you so you wouldn't have to admit you wanted it."

Nick's throat tightened.

He stumbled against a tree.

The bark scraped his elbow.

But he didn't feel it.

All he could feel was the throb between his legs—the sudden, shameful pulse of arousal.

He was hard.

Already.

She saw it.

Of course she saw it.

Her eyes dipped to the tent in his pants, and she smiled like a cat watching a mouse beg for mercy.

She crouched in front of him, inches away, her scent rolling over him—earth, sweat, and something darker. Something mineral and wet. Something like the first time you bleed.

"I can make it stop," she said, gently cupping the bulge through his jeans. "All of it. The guilt. The hiding. The story you tell yourself."

He gasped at the contact. He wanted to pull away—but he didn't.

"You don't know what I want," he whispered.

"I know everything. I've been inside you."

She stood and leaned closer and pressed her lips to his.

They were warm.

Softer than they had any right to be.

Her tongue slipped into his mouth with impossible control—like it had rehearsed this a thousand times. She kissed him deeply, slowly. His lips parted instinctively.

He moaned before he could stop himself.

That's when her hand unbuttoned his pants.

One flick. One tug.

They dropped.

She slid her fingers around his shaft.

Nick's head hit the tree.

"Stop," he breathed.

She stroked once.

Then twice.

"You're already mine," she whispered.

"I can't—"

"You already are."

His cock stood straight, obeying, twitching in her hand.

"Let me love you," she whispered. "The way no one else can."

The witch of the woods dropped to her knees.

His cock obeyed the witch and sprang free—erect, flushed, leaking.

She leaned forward and took him into her mouth.

Warm. Wet. Perfect suction.

She moved slowly at first, bobbing in rhythm, her lips sliding from base to tip and back again. Her tongue curled underneath. Her cheeks hollowed.

It was… impossible.

Her tongue was wrapping around his rock hard cock like a spring. No one had ever done it like this. Not even Robin.

And that thought—that guilt—made it hotter.

Nick groaned, his fists balling in the moss.

Also, power was at play. A monster, a demon of the woods was bobbing her beautiful head on his cock. She was submitting to him. The Witch of the woods was serving him. There's nothing hotter than this... he thought.

"Fuck…" he can't hold back now.

She moaned as she worked, the vibration rattling through him.

Her nails dug gently into his thighs.

He was losing himself.

Shame warred with pleasure—but the pleasure was winning.

Then she stopped.

She pulled back, licking her lips.

"You taste like confusion," she said. "I crave that."

Then she stood.

And something changed.

Her jawline had hardened slightly. Her shoulders... are they broader? Arms... a little more muscular? More masculine perhaps? But still, she had super smooth, silky skin, and those perfect tits.

Then he saw it.

Between her legs.

It emerged slowly, like a serpent rising.

Smooth, dark, obsidian-black.

A cock—long, curved, impossibly sleek. Veined with faint glowing cracks, like cooling magma. It pulsed gently, as if alive on its own. It was flesh, but it looked like stone.

Nick's eyes widened.

His breath caught.

"No."

"Yes."

"I'm not—"

"You are now."

She stepped forward, pushing his head down. His legs gave way. He had no strength to stand. There he was, kneeling before the witch. Helpless.

"Oh God no..." he thought.

She ran her fingers through his hair, guiding the tip to his lips.

"Open," she whispered.

Nick stared at the throbbing head- a mere inch away. "I will not."

"You already did."

Her hand pressed the shaft against his mouth.

The heat of it burned like sun-warmed stone.

He turned his head—but she moved with him.

Pressed again.

And this time—he parted his lips.

Just barely.

The tip slid past.

He gagged, reflexively.

She moaned. "That's it."

Her hands gripped his head harder.

She began to thrust—gently at first, just enough to stretch his mouth wider. The obsidian cock slid deeper each time, pressing against his throat. Tears formed in his eyes. Saliva spilled from the corners of his lips.

Each motion opened him further.

His lips stretched wide.

She thrust deeper.

And he took it.

Eyes fluttering. Heart pounding.

The shame was blinding.

But he was hard as stone.

She never looked away.

"You were always going to end up here," she said. "On your knees. Mouth full of cock."

"Mmmm-hmmm," he surprised himself with that response. "Did I know it?"

Then he moaned.

The shame... was electric.

She rocked her hips faster.

And he took it.

All of it.

The rhythm escalated. He was happily bobbing on her cock now. The contour, the hard flesh, the fact that he was submitting to her now. He was pleasuring HER, a god. His chest exploded with joy from the inside.

She pulled out with a wet pop, strings of saliva hanging from his lips.

"You're ready," she said.

Nick fell forward, coughing, gasping.

He didn't say anything.

Because part of him didn't want her to stop.

She gently lifted him up and spun him away from her with ease. His head was spinning. Unaware what was happening.

Pressed him against the tree.

Her hand gripped his ass—rough, demanding.

He feigned alarm, but didn't fight.

She lifted one of his legs slightly, just enough.

She placed her rock hard cock in between his ass cheeks. Not intrusive at first, but informative. This was happening. The demon gently slid it up and down a bit. It felt funny, but he craved it.

Then, a position change.

He felt the tip at his entrance.

No warning.

No mercy.

She pushed in.

It burned.

He cried out—his hands clawing at the bark.

But she didn't stop.

Her hips moved.

She fucked him.

Slow. Powerful.

The obsidian cock drove deeper, stretching him, opening him in ways no man had ever imagined.

She grunted with each thrust, hands on his hips, pounding him with primal rhythm. She was smiling with wild eyes a fire. She has conquered another.

Nick sobbed—but not from pain.

From release.

From shame so overwhelming it became *holy*.

"Say my name," she whispered in his ear.

He couldn't.

She slapped his ass. "Say it."

"Spearfinger," he moaned.

"Louder."

"Spearfinger!"

She drove harder.

THUMP.

THUMP.

THUMP.

The assault on Nick's ass cheeks echoed through the woods.

The forest warped around them—trees bending, fog swirling, air thickening with musk and rot and lust.

Robin's name tried to rise in his throat—but it wouldn't come.

Only *hers*.

His cock bounced with every thrust, dripping onto the moss.

He couldn't hold it anymore.

He exploded—hard—spurting onto the tree, his legs shaking.

Spearfinger groaned and slammed herself into him one final time.

She released. God knows what otherworldly concoction was unloaded into his insides... but there was a huge amount of it. It was warm. And he loved it.

Then she pulled out slowly. That felt great too. He whimpered with rapture.

Nick collapsed.

She stood over him, cock still glistening, smiling with satisfaction.

"Again, my boy... you submit." she said.

He curled on his side, broken.

Panting.

And somewhere far away...

Robin called his name.

CHAPTER 33
3000 Words

The moss beneath him clung to his skin when he woke.

Cold. Damp. Shameful.

Nick didn't move at first.

His pants were still around his ankles. His shirt had ridden up past his ribs. His arms were crossed over his chest, not for warmth—but for cover. The ache in his thighs was sharp. The dull pressure inside him pulsed with every shift of breath.

The forest was quiet.

Almost soft.

There were feathers again—**raven feathers**—all around him. They framed his body like petals. A wreath of silence. A witness.

He didn't remember falling asleep.

He remembered **her.**

And the way he moaned when she entered him.

The way he begged.

The way he came.

His fingers curled in the moss, digging small trenches.

He sat up slowly, pain rippling through his core.

He pulled his pants up with trembling hands, still slick with sweat and forest debris. He didn't cry. He didn't vomit. He just stared straight ahead.

Trying not to think about the fact that part of him wanted to feel it again.

Robin's footsteps were light when they came.

She appeared through the trees like a ghost, her shirt now nearly shredded, her legs scratched and bleeding. Her face—tired. Hollow-eyed. Lips dry. She froze when she saw him.

He froze too.

For a long moment, neither said a word.

Then Robin stepped forward.

Her voice cracked.

"What happened?"

Nick rubbed his jaw. "I... I got lost."

"No," she said. "What happened?"

"I told you. I—"

"Cut the shit, Nick." Her voice didn't rise. That made it worse. "You're filthy. You smell like sweat and sex. Your pants were down. I saw you before you moved."

Nick looked down.

"I fell," he mumbled.

Robin crouched beside him.

Her hand reached out—but didn't touch.

Her eyes were searching his. Probing.

"Was it her?" she asked.

He hesitated. Too long.

"No."

Robin stared.

"She didn't come to you again?"

"No."

"You didn't see her?"

"No."

"You didn't touch her?"

"No."

"Did she touch you?"

"No."

Robin's jaw clenched.

"You're lying."

"I'm not."

"You are," she said. "Because I know what you look like when you lie. You can't make eye contact. You repeat yourself. Your mouth curls at the edge. And right now—every box is checked."

Nick turned away.

"I'm tired," he said.

Robin stood.

She didn't walk away.

She just stood there for a long time.

Watching him.

Like a wolf trying to decide if it's worth the trouble to bite.

Then she finally said, "I hope you're telling the truth."

He didn't respond.

Because he knew he wasn't.

They moved through the trees slowly.

Robin stayed several steps ahead, silent except for her footsteps.

Nick didn't try to catch up.

His stomach churned. His ass still ached. His head felt like it was full of ash.

The sky darkened as they traveled.

They passed an old stone chimney—a remnant of a burned cabin long gone. Robin paused beside it.

"Let's rest here," she said.

She sat on a moss-covered root and closed her eyes.

Nick dropped beside her, pressing his back to the cool stone.

For a while, neither said anything.

Then Robin turned.

"I'm scared," she said.

He nodded. "Me too."

"I keep thinking… maybe I'm not all the way back. Maybe she's still inside me."

"You're not her."

"And maybe you're not you anymore."

His throat tightened.

Robin pulled her knees to her chest.

"You didn't used to lie," she whispered.

That's when she saw something.

Her eyes shifted.

She rose slowly, walked to the edge of the chimney.

Three white squares lay in the dirt.

Polaroids.

Robin bent down.

Nick didn't see what she was looking at.

Not yet.

She picked them up.

One by one.

Her hands started to shake.

Then she turned.

Her face was blank. Too blank.

"What are these?" she asked.

He didn't answer.

She held them up.

The first: **Robin, no wait... that's Spearfinger**—naked—her lips around Nick's cock. Hair tied back. Kneeling in the moss.

Eyes closed. Mouth full.

The second: **Nick**—kneeling before Spearfinger, lips wrapped around her obsidian shaft, hands resting on her hips.

The third: **Spearfinger behind Nick**, cock buried deep. His mouth open mid-moan. Her arms wrapped around his chest, holding him like a lover.

In every photo—every single one—**they looked like they were in love**.

Smiling. Locked into each other. Intimate.

Robin stared at him.

Then back at the photos.

"You lied to me," she said softly.

"What are those?"

"Did you think I'd never find out?"

"Now listen, you can't trust what you see in those photos, you know that. Now what are-."

She laughed.

It wasn't a kind laugh.

"Why are you smiling in every one of these?"

"What are you looking at?"

"You know, you fucking asshole."

Nick's eyes burned.

"She seduced me... with magic. I was scared. I was weak. I—"

"You *loved* it," Robin snapped.

"I didn't."

"Then why is your face in the third one the same face you make when you come with me?"

He had no answer.

She tossed the photos at him.

They fluttered down like dead birds.

"You fucked her," she whispered. "You *loved* fucking her."

"I was possessed."

"You look like you're in love."

Nick's fists clenched.

Robin circled him slowly.

"You've been waiting your whole life for permission to feel something like that. You just never had the guts to ask."

"That's not fair."

"You cheated on me."

"So did you!"

She pressed a finger into his chest.

"You know what's funny?" she said. "I actually believed in you. I believed you loved me. And maybe you did. But whatever that was—it's over now. You gave it to her."

"I didn't give her anything."

She stepped back.

"Yes, you did. You gave her your *soul.*"

That night, they didn't share the fire.

Robin slept with her back to him, arms folded tight, the shredded shirt barely covering her.

Nick sat alone, knees to his chest, the Polaroids still on the ground beside him.

He didn't burn them.

He couldn't.

He stared at the images long into the dark, the smiles haunting him more than anything else in the woods.

The next morning, she didn't say goodbye.

She just walked away.

And this time…

He didn't follow.

CHAPTER 34
Always in His Hair

Nick hadn't moved in hours. He was starving. But he didn't think about food.

The forest didn't ask him to. It let him sit, slumped beneath a leaning oak whose roots rose up like crooked ribs. His back was pressed into the bark. His pants still felt dirty. His thighs still sore. But it wasn't pain that occupied his thoughts now.

It was **her**.

Spearfinger.

He stared at the moss in front of him, not really seeing it.

The shame had dulled.

The fear, too.

What was left was something worse.

Something he didn't want to name.

Longing.

The sex—the act—should've broken him. Should've destroyed any trace of desire. But instead…

He kept replaying it.

Not the violence.

Not the horror.

The other parts.

The warmth of her lips.

The feel of her tongue as she sucked him.

The way she looked into his eyes when she took him.

She hadn't looked at him like prey.

She'd looked at him like he *mattered*.

Like she saw something beautiful in him, even as she split him apart.

Robin had never looked at him that way.

No one had.

He touched his lip—still swollen from where she'd kissed him too hard.

He swallowed thickly.

He hated himself.

But he wanted to see her again.

Not to fight.

Not to resist.

He wanted her to hold him. He wanted to fuck her. He wanted her to Fuck him again. Take him apart.

His stomach flipped. He felt like a teenager.

He had a **crush**.

Like a girl in a notebook scribbling *Mrs. Spearfinger* in little hearts.

He barked out a laugh.

It sounded hollow. Weak.

But still—his cock twitched at the thought of her.

"Jesus Christ," he muttered.

He rolled onto his side and curled up. A breeze passed overhead. Somewhere, a raven cawed.

The forest shifted.

He thought he heard her name whispered by the wind.

Spearfinger.

And deep down, he hoped she was still watching.

Elsewhere in the woods...

Trevor was running.

Or walking.

Or stumbling.

It all blurred together.

His jeans were torn. His arms were bleeding from a hundred scratches. Sweat clung to every inch of him, soaking his chest, plastering his hair to his scalp.

He hadn't eaten in days.

Maybe weeks.

Time was a fucked-up thing now to everyone mortal in these woods.

He still had the Polaroid in his back pocket—the one showing his own corpse.

He hadn't looked at it in hours, but he could feel it there. Burning through the denim like it knew its truth would come soon.

And then there was the **other** Polaroid.

The one he *hadn't* shown the others.

The one of **Emma**.

She was standing in the woods.

Just... *off.*

Her eyes were too big. Too dark. Her mouth curled in a way that didn't look like a smile—but like someone *remembering* what smiling felt like.

He didn't know where the photo came from.

It was just there one morning.

Tucked into his boot.

Emma. Alive. Maybe.

Maybe not.

"Daddy…"

He froze.

The voice echoed behind him.

Soft.

Childlike.

He turned.

Nothing.

Just vines and fog.

He ran a hand down his face.

"No," he said out loud. "Not real. You're not real."

But the voice came again.

"Daddy… help me…"

Trevor clenched his fists. He wasn't her dad, he was the fun uncle, but how does he tell her... that her daddy is dead?

His eyes scanned the trees.

And then—

A flash of **pink** caught his eye.

Fabric.

He crept forward and found it.

A tiny dress.

Faded. Torn.

Emma's.

The same one she wore in a photo that used to sit on his mantle. From Dollywood. Smiling next to a guy in a foam bear suit.

He grabbed it and fell to his knees.

His chest shook.

Tears threatened to come, but he held them back.

"Where are you…" he whispered.

The wind shifted again.

The raven cawed from above.

He looked up—and saw it.

Perched high.

Black eyes watching him.

"You know," he muttered.

The raven tilted its head.

He stood slowly, clutching the dress.

"Take me to her."

Back at the oak, Nick sat up as the light changed.

A storm was coming.

The wind smelled electric.

He stood and stretched. His back cracked. His ass still hurt—but it was a good hurt now.

Familiar.

Welcomed.

He hated that he thought that.

He started walking. No idea where.

His boots squelched in mud. The forest grew thicker. The trees started leaning in again—closer together. Watching.

He came to a clearing filled with broken rocks, shaped almost like seats. Natural, but too deliberate.

At the center, something shimmered.

Not a creature.

A **feeling**.

Desire.

Nick stepped forward.

Then stopped.

A small, square shape lay in the grass.

He bent down.

Another Polaroid.

He flipped it.

It wasn't of him.

It was of *her*.

Spearfinger. Mid-transformation. Her lips parted. Her breasts exposed. Impossibly wide hips. That curved black cock glowing faintly beneath her.

And written across the bottom, in what looked like dried blood:

YOU MISS ME

He pocketed it and smiled.

"Does she miss me?"

CHAPTER 35
The New Girl in Town

The woods had stopped trying to lie.

There were no more twisting trails or misdirected moss. The forest had become what it truly was: a stage. And Nick was center. The sun was seemingly low in the sky. He had no idea what day this was, what time this was, what year this was. This was a real life dream.

He walked in silence.

The memory of her—the way she filled him, consumed him, *remade* him—haunted every step. He tried to resist the pulse in his blood, the ache in his bones. But it was there. Real. Gnawing.

At this moment, Robin was a distant memory.

She hadn't said goodbye. Hadn't even cursed him one last time. Just vanished, like the forest had swallowed her on her behalf. And he didn't follow. He couldn't. Because the thing drawing him now was deeper.

Older.

Her.

He reached a clearing rimmed by burned stumps and dead flowers. At its center: a wide stone slab, overgrown with black moss. It pulsed faintly beneath the skin of the earth, like a buried heart.

And she was there.

Waiting.

Spearfinger stood with her arms outstretched, black hair blowing despite the still air. Her body gleamed—bare, perfect, awful. Her mouth curled into a knowing smile.

"You came back to see me!" she said like a regular girl in young love would.

Nick eyes grew. Pure excitement. But didn't answer. He had... butterflies?

He stepped toward her slowly, shame wrapped around him like a blanket.

She tilted her head.

"Still ashamed?"

He nodded.

"Still hard?"

He didn't need to nod.

She walked to him, her voice low and smooth.

"Do you know why you feel this way?" she whispered. "Why you can't stop thinking about what happened? Why even now—after everything—you still want me?"

Nick's hands shook.

"I don't know what I want," he muttered.

"Yes, you do," she said. "Because I've been inside you."

She pressed her hand to his chest.

"No one ever loved you the right way," she whispered. "Not your mother. Not your lovers. Not Robin. You've been pretending. Wearing your body like armor."

Her other hand slid down to his stomach. Her fingers sparked against him, heat and cold at once.

"But I touched the deepest part of you. I'm still in there. In the thick of that nasty tar. Your shame. I know what you want."

Nick's lips parted.

"Say it," she breathed.

He shook his head.

She leaned in, her lips against his ear.

"You want to shed this hairy, muscular skin."

He gasped.

"You want to be *fucked* as a woman."

His knees buckled.

"What? No... I..."

"I can give you that," she said. "The truth of who you are. I can shape you into what you've always dreamed of, in the part of your brain you never dared open."

Nick tried to run.

But his legs betrayed him.

The moss swallowed his boots.

He fell forward onto the slab.

And then—

Her hand reached down and touched his chest. It was burning.

The world pulsed.

His ribs cracked.

He screamed as they shrank slightly.

His spine shifted. Muscles tore and reknit. His arms snapped inward, bones reshaping into lithe, feminine curves.

His hair darkened, lengthened, spilled down over his shoulders in thick black waves.

His waist cinched.

His ass swelled.

His thighs thickened like stone softened in fire.

His nipples ached—then tingled—then bloomed into soft pink buds, flush against the chill.

He arched and moaned, voice no longer his own.

His hands flew to his face—cheekbones now sharper, lips fuller, jaw gone. Goatee gone.

Spearfinger stood above him, watching him convulse in the moss.

"You're beautiful," she whispered.

"No—" he cried, in a voice higher, smoother.

Eventually, Nick stopped moving for a little while. He was sore. He sat up, his clothes dangled off of his body. His tits holding his T-shirt up, his shorts didn't fit right, but his new fat ass was keeping them where they should be, for now.

He reached over to his back pack. He noticed his tiny, smooth arms with black fingernails. It made his head dizzy. When he reached it, his phone was long dead, but he was trying to catch a glimpse of himself in the dark screen. What did she do?

What he saw almost gave him a panic attack. A young goth girl. He used to watch girls like this for hours on his phone with lust. "To be with one of those girls. TO BE one of those girls", he used to think, coveting their bodies in the deepest recesses of himself. He always wanted to see what it would be like. Now he was one... but for how long? What's going to happen?

"Stand up"

He obeyed.

Nick's shoes fell off and he tried to stand. But his body was like a newborn baby giraffe. He stood barefoot in the pine needles, his new form trembling in the moonlight. His thick, smooth thighs were streaked with sweat and dirt. Jet black hair spilled around her pale face like oil slicks. His dirty T-shirt barely contained his soft pink nipples, which had become impossibly sensitive since the change. His camouflage cargo shorts barely clung to his new curves, his wide hips framed by the shadows of oak and ash.

He could still taste Spearfinger on his lips from before.

"Do you see yourself now?" Spearfinger asked. Her obsidian eyes glowed faintly, and her body shimmered with ancient heat. Her bare feet didn't touch the ground. Her face still wore Robin's smile, but her body was something else: half goddess, half nightmare, fully beautiful.

Nick's breath caught.

"I didn't ask for this," he said. But his voice cracked. His knees nearly buckled.

"You begged for it. In your dreams. In your shame."

Spearfinger reached out with her hand—and traced the curve of Nick's cheek. "You asked me to show you what you were."

Nick couldn't remember if he did, but at this point, he didn't care. It was full surrender time. He whimpered as the finger slid down his throat, between the swell of his new breasts, and hooked under the T-shirt.

"Take it off," Spearfinger said.

Nick obeyed.

He ripped the shirt off over his head and stared back at Spearfinger. His breasts bouncing free in the cold air. He tried to cover them, but Spearfinger growled—low and disapproving—so Nick let his arms fall to his sides. The wind caught his long black hair. The leaves swirled around them like dancers.

Spearfinger kissed him.

It was not tender.

It was dominance incarnate—teeth, tongue, command.

Nick melted. He opened his mouth and let Spearfinger in, his new body already aching in ways he has never felt before. Spearfinger's free hand cupped the back of his head while the other slid down his belly and between his legs, pressing through the moist maw.

Nick gasped.

"You're soaked," Spearfinger whispered. "Your body remembers me."

Nick half laughed. He wants nothing more than this, right now.

Spearfinger dropped the camo shorts with an expert tug, and then sank two fingers into Nick. Nick arched, moaning, one leg lifting instinctively. His moans were higher now, throatier. He hated how natural it felt. This is changing everything. These new sensations, overwhelming his nervous system, were firing synapses of joy throughout his new body.

Spearfinger drove him back into a tree, pinned him there, and began to kiss down his chest. Her tongue flicked over Nick's nipple, then bit it—hard. Nick cried out. Not in pain. In complete surrender.

"You love this," Spearfinger said, lapping at the bite mark. "You wanted to be taken. Now you are."

"Yes!"

Spearfinger's hand, now completely obsidian, hovered near Nick's lips.

"Kiss it," Spearfinger said.

Nick did.

He kissed the stone fingers. Then opened his mouth and took one in, sucking on it as his hips bucked against the other hand working him from below.

"I'm yours," Nick whispered.

"No," Spearfinger growled. "You're mine."

Nick screamed as he came, his new body shuddering, his new thighs clenched around Spearfinger's hand. The woods echoed with his climax. Birds scattered from the trees. The wind itself seemed to hush.

Spearfinger held him until the trembling stopped.

Then, as Nick sagged against her, Spearfinger lifted her face.

Robin was watching.

From the brush. Silent. Pale. Eyes wide.

And Spearfinger smiled—never looking away from Robin—as she kissed Nick again.

Spearfinger lifted up the avatar off the ground. They continued to kiss. Spearfinger taunting Robin at this point.

When Nick opened his eyes, the demon was already lowering him gently back against the stone.

His new body trembled—alien and electric.

She climbed on top of him.

And slid apart his legs with her thighs.

His pussy gushed. Spine twisted involuntarily. Nipples hardened. Breasts heaved. It was erotic, terrifying, exciting, joyful, evil... and his head was still spinning in this new frame and from the orgasms he was already gifted.

And Spearfinger leaned down until her lips brushed his ear.

"Now let me show you what you've always needed."

And she did.

From the trees, Robin watched.

She hadn't meant to follow.

She had only wanted distance.

But the forest had turned, and the paths betrayed her, until she found herself here—watching from behind a dead tree.

At first, she didn't recognize the girl on the slab.

But then she saw the discarded clothes on the forest floor.

They were Nick's.

His eyes wide with confusion.

Then with pleasure.

And Robin understood.

Her hand covered her mouth, but it didn't stop the sob.

She watched as Spearfinger mounted this new girl—his body writhing, his face lit with something more than lust. More than surrender.

Joy.

She watched Nick's new hands clutch the stone. Then his hands searching and finding Spearfinger's perfect tits. Spearfinger also started playing with these new, smaller tits with pink, soft nipples. Then, the deep tongue kissing. The writhing with joy. Watched his new thick legs spread wide. Watched him cry out over and over.

It was unmistakable.

He was having **orgasms**.

More than one.

Deep. Full. Shuddering.

Each one twisting his face into something between bliss and agony.

Bang.

Bang.

Bang.

Spearfinger was in full machine fuck mode now. Nick's eyes crossed. Spearfinger grabbed Nick's soft pink tongue with two fingers, yanked it out of his mouth, and held it as she rammed this young virgin into otherworldly bliss with her magical obsidian cock. Orgasm after orgasm. The moaning was loud and long and primal.

To Robin, this was a nightmare.

Robin stumbled back.

Fell to her knees.

She wanted to scream.

But there was no sound.

Just that image burning into her brain.

On the slab, Nick collapsed.

Sweat soaked the curls of black hair now stuck to his cheek. His breasts rose and fell in heavy gasps.

Spearfinger leaned down and kissed him softly.

"There you are," she said. "Now you'll never have to pretend again."

Nick tried to speak.

But nothing came.

His new body trembled with the memory of every touch.

Every burst of heat.

He was whole.

And hollow.

And terrified.

And in love.

Nick's youthful body reached up for Spearfinger innocently, and to Robin's horror, Spearfinger obliged. The witch wrapped her muscular arms around this girl version of Nick and held him like new lovers do. They held the embrace for a long time.

After what felt like an eternity, Spearfinger slowly turned her head with the empty eyes, and stared right into Robin's soul. The witch smiled an evil smile-Nick's reborn, supple body still shaking with safety and rapture.

CHAPTER 36
Emma

They walked in silence, Emma in front, Trevor just behind her.

Her bare feet didn't seem to feel the roots or the cold. Her hair was tangled with leaves, and the oversized flannel shirt she wore—Butch's, Trevor realized—hung off her shoulders like it didn't belong to her.

The same could be said for everything about her.

Her gait was too smooth.

Her breath too quiet.

Her presence... unsettling.

And yet—it was *Emma*. She looked like Emma. Sounded like Emma. The way she turned back every few yards to see if he was still following. The way her eyes flickered with quiet pain. The way her voice caught just slightly when she said his name.

"Uncle Trevor," she had whispered when he first found her, curled near a tree, eyes wide and wet, "You're not dead."

Neither are you, he thought. But he hadn't said it out loud.

Because part of him wasn't sure.

"Where are we going, sweetheart?" Trevor asked, trying to keep his voice light.

Emma didn't turn around.

"You'll see."

The words dropped like stones.

She stepped over a patch of black moss. He noticed it curled away from her skin like it didn't want to touch her.

Trevor tightened the grip on his machete.

Not to use it.

Just to remember it was real.

He hadn't said anything about Butch.

Not yet.

"You hungry?" he asked.

Emma shook her head.

"Thirsty?"

"No."

"You sure?"

She stopped.

Turned to face him.

Her eyes were a little too wide. Too dry.

"Why do you keep asking me that stuff?" she said.

"I'm worried about you."

"I'm fine."

"You were gone a long time."

Emma blinked. "Time is different here."

She turned again and kept walking.

Trevor let her go a few steps before following.

CHAPTER 37
Blame the Woods

Spearfinger smiled at Robin like she'd just stolen something—and she had.

Wrapped around the trembling girl-shaped body on the slab, she cooed once more into Nick's ear, then raised his head and locked eyes with Robin in the trees.

"You're too late," she said, her voice velvet over glass. "He... She's mine."

And then she vanished.

Not like a ghost.

Like smoke sucked backward into the sky.

Robin stepped from the trees slowly, heart hammering.

Nick—no, *Nikki*—was still curled on the stone slab, body glistening with sweat, chest heaving. Long black hair clung to her cheek.

But as Robin took one more step forward—

The transformation reversed.

Hard. And it was painful.

It started in the chest.

Nikki—Nick—arched with a scream as his breasts flattened and his ribs cracked outward.

His waist thickened. His hips and thighs shrank. His voice dropped back into a trembling baritone.

Hair shortened. Nails broke. Lips thinned.

He moaned in agony as his bones re-formed under skin that had only just adjusted.

When it was over, Nick lay naked, gasping, arms curled around his stomach.

His goatee had returned like a scar.

And so had his dick.

Robin stared down at him, wide-eyed, saying nothing.

Nick pushed himself upright slowly.

He didn't look at her.

"That was weird, wasn't it?" he laughed.

Robin's lip curled. "You were moaning like a porn star."

Nick looked at her, his eyes red.

"Yep. I was. I was scary and weird and icky and I felt like Hell during some of it."

"Some of it?" Robin gasped.

"I never cheated on you before. I feel bad about that. I really do. But... I liked it," he said. "I miss it already."

Robin stepped back. "You miss being a girl?"

"I miss how it *felt*." He gestured to his chest. "Everything was… electric. Like every nerve was alive. Like I was *real* for the first time. And oh my God- the orgasms-"

"Oh Nick. Shut the fuck up. Don't talk to me about orgasms that you had with that murderous witch." Robin's voice cracked. "She's using you! You were a *doll*."

"I would be her doll anytime."

"Oh my god! This is a nightmare!"

He stood up—bare, shaking.

"I didn't ask for this!" he shouted. "I didn't *plan* to feel this way! I don't want any of this to be real. I want to go home!"

Robin's arms crossed. "So what are you now? Trans?"

"No. Maybe? I don't know..."

"Are you gay?"

"No... I find men gross... Except for..."

"Except for what?"

"The cock. That... I think... I think I like a lot," Nick laughed.

Robin scoffed.

He broke.

"One time, when I was sixteen, I saved up for a giant dildo. Ordered it online. Lied and said it was a gag gift for a girl when it came in the mail."

Robin winced.

"I *used* it," he whispered. "I *liked* it. Several times. I threw it away because I hated it. Then, eventually, I won enough playing cards to order another one."

Robin shook her head. "Jesus, Nick."

"I'm not happy about this."

"*That's* your confession?"

He looked at her.

"I think I liked being a woman just now more than I've ever liked being myself."

She flinched like he'd hit her.

"Then go back to her," she snapped. "Go beg that evil, cannibalistic, murderous Spearfinger for another ride."

"I would in a second."

Robin's face hardened.

He didn't stop.

"Because she made me feel *seen*. Like I wasn't disgusting. Like everything I buried my whole life was… was *supposed* to be there."

"Fuck this."

Robin turned to walk away.

Then they both froze.

A rhythmic thumping sound echoed through the trees.

Wet.

Sticky.

Animal.

They turned.

And saw it.

Bestiality the wrestler was hunched in the clearing, wrestling trunks around his ankles, humping the Bear furry from the elevator dream from behind. The Bear furry was thrusting into another furry not from the elevator—it looked like a girl fox maybe— who was pressed up against a tree.

All of them groaned in sync.

A symphony of stupid, filthy bliss.

Nick stared, jaw open.

Robin covered her mouth.

"What the actual *fuck*," she whispered.

Then Bestiality the wrestler turned and beckoned at Nick.

Nick took a step forward.

Robin grabbed his arm. "You're not seriously—?"

"I don't know!" he cried.

He looked down at his hand. It was shaking.

"I don't know who I am right now!"

Robin's voice cracked. "You were about to join them! That sick furry shit?"

"They look like they are having fun*!*"

"They look like a deleted scene from hell!"

Nick turned away from the furry sex scene, laughing and sobbing all at once.

"I swear it's the *woods,*" he said, clutching his head.

Robin stared at him—broken, filthy, naked. His dick is semi hard again.

She didn't say a word.

The furry orgy continued behind them.

And Nick sat there, staring at the dirt, whispering:

"It's the woods. It's the woods. It's the woods…"

Robin was through.

CHAPTER 38
The Body in the Hollow

Trevor followed Emma through the trees, the mist thickening around them.

Her hand held his gently, fingers small and warm. She hadn't spoken in a while. Just walked, silent and slow, like she was leading a horse to water.

He didn't ask again where they were going.

Part of him didn't want to know.

Something was wrong. Something had *been* wrong.

But she looked like Emma.

Sounded like her.

So he followed.

Because if he stopped, he'd have to admit she wasn't real.

That maybe she hadn't been for some time.

They came to a hollow surrounded by jagged rocks.

The trees here were different—gray and split, their bark stripped down to nerve-white wood. Moss hung like rotten fur. The wind didn't blow. The air held its breath.

At the center of the hollow was a shape.

Trevor slowed.

Emma let go of his hand.

She turned to him and said, "There she is."

Trevor blinked.

"What?"

She pointed toward the shape.

Trevor stepped forward.

His boots squelched in blood-soaked moss.

He saw her.

The real Emma.

Her body lay twisted in the underbrush. Her mouth open, eyes cloudy, arms chewed by animals. Her stomach—

Gone.

Cleanly carved open.

And her **liver**—

Missing.

The realization hit like a rock in his throat.

"No…"

He dropped to his knees beside her.

"No, baby girl, no—"

He touched her face.

Cold.

He turned to the girl behind him, his voice trembling.

"Who are you?"

The girl smiled.

Her eyes blackened.

Her skin cracked down the center like a porcelain mask.

And she stepped forward.

With each step, her frame shifted.

Grew.

Twisted.

Her hair lengthened.

Her lips thickened.

And the child was gone.

In her place stood **Spearfinger**.

Full height. Full glory. Glowing with power.

Her skin shimmered like obsidian soaked in blood.

"Emma's been gone a long time," she said.

Trevor stood, backing away.

"You bitch," he whispered.

"I wore her skin for a while," Spearfinger said. "It felt... sweet."

Ravens landed around them in a sudden flurry.

Six. Then nine. Then a dozen.

They gathered around Emma's corpse.

And **fed**.

Tearing at her insides with wet, satisfied caws.

Spearfinger spread her arms and spun like a child in a field.

"They remember the taste," she said. "And so do I."

Trevor raised his machete.

Spearfinger laughed.

"You think you're special, Uncle Trevor?"

"I'm not going down like Butch."

"No," she said, stepping close. "You'll go down **better**."

She lunged.

The machete came up.

It hit her arm—and bounced off with a spark.

She caught it mid-air, twisted it from his grip, and tossed it.

Then she grabbed his neck and lifted him from the ground like he was nothing.

"Ever seen your own liver?" she whispered.

He choked.

Her obsidian finger sharpened mid-air—long, black, humming with power.

She dragged it slowly along his side, just beneath his ribs.

He screamed.

She cut deeper.

His vision blurred.

His knees kicked, trying to find earth.

She sliced him open with surgical grace.

Reached inside.

And pulled out his **liver**—steaming and red and pulsing.

Trevor gasped once.

Then nothing.

The ravens cawed louder.

Spearfinger dropped his body onto the moss beside Emma.

She lifted the liver to her lips.

Bit.

Chewed.

Moaned.

"I'm getting stronger," she said through her smile.

One of the ravens flew onto her shoulder and began picking at the edges of the liver.

She didn't stop it.

The others circled.

Blood dripped from her chin.

Her eyes burned like coals.

"I'll eat them all," she whispered to the wind. "Until the woods are mine again."

And the forest, ancient and silent, said nothing to stop her.

CHAPTER 39
The Ceremony of Flesh

Robin's lips were cracked. Nick's shirt was shredded and clinging to him with old sweat. Their bodies were brittle with dehydration, and their stomachs had long since stopped growling—there was nothing left to growl for.

"We should've been out by now," Robin whispered.

Nick nodded. "I stopped trying to guess how long it's been. I've given up hope. Starvation aside, I'm starting to feel normal again. When I think about what has happ-."

"I don't care right now. I just want a cheeseburger."

Nick smiled, weakly.

The wind blew harder here. Clean. Distant. The forest below stretched like a writhing ocean of green. Behind them, it pulsed with unseen whispers.

Robin reached into her bag and pulled out the **mojo**—the totem that had haunted them, beckoned to Spearfinger, drawn her like a fly to heat.

She held it in her palm.

"What if this is the reason everything went to shit?" she said.

Nick stared at it. The carved face, the tangled twine, the crusted beads.

"We burn it?"

"No," Robin said. "We throw it off the cliff."

Nick looked at her.

"We don't know what that'll do. I'm scared to think. I think we burn it."

"I don't have the tools, the strength or the will to burn it. We don't know what *keeping* it is doing. I hate it. I hate what its done. I hate what it has done to me, to you... to us. I'm so sorry, Nick."

"I'm sorry too, babe," Nick responded.

Robin stood.

Walked to the edge.

Held the totem over the drop.

The woods behind them rustled—like it was watching.

"I'm done being someone's puppet," she said.

And she **threw** it.

It spun twice in the air.

And vanished into the trees below.

Robin stepped back, trembling.

Nothing happened.

No explosion. No wind. No scream.

Just silence.

They walked for hours.

At first, there was hope.

The forest didn't shift.

No new trails appeared.

Things felt normal.

But then the sun dipped behind the trees again—*too fast*.

Robin stumbled once.

Then again.

Her mouth was white at the corners.

Nick stopped helping her, because he couldn't even help himself anymore.

They were soon going to die out here. They were starving.

They dropped beneath an old tree. Nick remarked that this place looked familiar. Maybe they are finding their way out.

"I'm so thirsty," Robin croaked.

After the last encounter with the demon, it seemed to them that the magic of the woods was wearing off. In one way, that was great news. In a real place, maybe they could find an exit, or help. But in another way, things were getting much worse. Their bodies were failing at what seemed like an accelerated pace.

That's when the wind stopped.

And they felt it.

That creeping hum.

That pull in the base of their skulls.

The **magic** had returned.

Robin looked up, eyes wide.

"Oh, God no—"

A shadow passed overhead.

Nick stood, even before he could understand why.

She descended like a cloud.

Floating.

Beautiful.

Terrible.

Spearfinger.

She hovered above the ground like the air wanted to carry her.

Her long black hair whipped around her. Her body was bare again, obsidian-smooth, hips gliding as she slowly touched down.

Around her neck hung the **mojo. She fucking found it**.

And on her lips—**blood**.

Fresh.

A smear down her chin like she didn't care to wipe it away.

Robin stood, weak but furious.

"You bitch," she growled.

Spearfinger smiled.

"Oh, sweetheart. Still mad?" She reached down and wiped the blood with two fingers, then licked them. "Your friend was delicious. So full of fear. So fatherly."

Robin trembled.

"You killed that guy..."

"Trevor joined the forest," Spearfinger said sweetly. "I just got done feeding him to my ravens and spreading him out like compost."

Robin asked "What the hell are you? What the hell do you want?"

Nick fell to his knees.

Like a man greeting God.

Spearfinger said, "Ask your boy. He seems to have the right idea."

Robin turned, horrified. "Nick—what the hell are you doing?"

He sobbed, eyes wide with ecstasy. "She's so beautiful."

"You said she *broke* you."

"I loved it," he cried out to Spearfinger.

Spearfinger stepped toward him, her feet never touching the ground.

"My beautiful boy," she purred. "Would you like to worship me again?"

Nick nodded violently.

Robin shouted, "Get up!"

He didn't.

Spearfinger undid the twine around her neck and dropped the mojo between her breasts. It landed on the ground. As this happened, her mysterious obsidian cock emerged and grew from between her legs. It straightened out like a circus balloon, became larger and larger, and then fully erect. It was only a few inches from Nick's eager mouth.

Then she lifted Nick's chin.

"Open, my pet," she whispered.

He did.

She stepped forward.

Robin watched as he pressed his face between her thighs, moaning like a priest giving penance, his head bobbing up and down like a cheap street hooker.

"No," Robin said again. "No, Nick... no, no. You've got to fight this! You can't let her win!!!"

"MMMMHMHHMM, " he responded.

But something was happening around Robin.

The trees began to move—just barely. Their rhythm pulsed with the same beat that thumped in Robin's skull. She grabbed the back of her head.

A low drum.

A heartbeat.

Magic.

Lust.

Robin backed up—and tripped.

She hit the moss hard and rolled over.

She shook her head. Massive headache. She saw Nick—still on his knees, head bobbing religiously, hands on Spearfinger's hips, *crying* tears of joy as he worshiped her.

And Robin's body—

Reacted.

Her nipples ached. Her throat tightened. Her thighs pressed together on instinct. She grinded her hips a little. A twitch down below. Then her pussy became wet.

She watched.

"Look at that bitch go. How hot," she thought.

Robin has sometimes fantasized about Nick being with other men. She envisioned it occasionally when she masturbated in the shower. She knew it was weird. She didn't like the thought of it very soon after she released. And she NEVER mentioned it to Nick before for fear of retaliation. Now here they are, it's no longer fantasy. He's gobbling a cock like a good little whore right in front of her. It's awful... but now... it's not so bad at all. Look at him go.

"Yeah, boy... get it." Her eyes widened. Robin licked her lips out of muscle memory.

Spearfinger reached out her hand.

Robin didn't take it.

Not at first.

But she stood.

And walked to them.

And then she surprised herself. She knelt. It was time to worship the goddess of the forest alongside of her boyfriend.

What followed was not human.

It wasn't even sexual.

It was **ritual**.

The three of them became motion. Heat. Wet skin and tangled hair and teeth. Spearfinger's body gleamed as it twisted around and between them, guiding their mouths, their hands, their hips.

Spearfinger smiled. They are hers. She has won.

Robin and Nick—once enemies, once lovers—found themselves **sharing** her.

They knelt before her, looking up into her eyes for approval. They started to kiss the erect cock playfully, but soon they were wrestling the penis away from each other, each deep throating it when they could. The owner of the mouth without the witch's cock buried deep inside of it, started acting like a jealous sibling, growing impatient and ripping the cock away from their fellow sex slave to deep throat the cock until the other couldn't stand being without it.

"Play nice, my pets," Spearfinger said, looking down while guiding their heads, almost in a motherly tone and fashion..

They looked up at her smiling face and agreed with their eyes. Then resumed.

They took turns pressing lips to her obsidian flesh and gobbling down. They eventually became playful with each other and the erect dick. Sticking it in each other's mouths, giggling, looking up for approval, sometimes filling their time by taking the witch's huge, full balls into their mouths.

There's no telling how long these two orally serviced their tormentor, but it had to be awhile.

Like robots, they symbiotically assumed positions.

Robin's gorgeous body got on all fours first, taking in Nick's cock with her pouty lips, her throat stuffed with apology, lust and Nick's delicious member. Spearfinger plunged herself into Robin's dripping wet pussy from behind. The forest legend grabbed Robin's amazing hips with both gnarled hands and went to work. They moved in rhythm with the forest. Pure nature connection. It was hot, but Nick stared into the eyes of Spearfinger longingly the entire time.

Then suddenly...

Another position change.

Robin sat on Nick's face while Spearfinger pushed into him from behind. He moaned with delight. The best of both worlds. As Spearfinger plunged herself deeper and deeper into Nick's body, she stuck her middle finger into Robin's asshole. The demon was making the couple moan with each thrust. Nick was busy experiencing being taken yet again, while plunging his tongue into and rediscovering Robin's wet folds. His face was soon the recipient of copious amounts of Robin's delicious nectar. Robin couldn't handle the magically enhanced pleasure. She grabbed her own tits and bit down on her lips, thrashing her head around, almost out of control.

***

The forest sang.

The trees bent toward them.

The ravens watched in silence.

When the final **climax** came, it was like a thunderclap.

Nick arched and screamed a muffled scream into Robin's pussy.

Robin liked that a lot, and she dug her nails into moss and wept.

Spearfinger tilted her head back and made the forest tremble with her as she sprayed into Nick.

They collapsed together.

A pile of heat and limbs and steam.

Robin laughed.

Nick laughed and cried simultaneously.

Spearfinger held them both, each resting their heads on her shoulders, burrowing into her perfect round tits, still flushed and huge. Smiles on each of their faces.

They were ruined.

And they were **happy**. They were all happy.

CHAPTER 40
Good Wood

It had become a low-hanging dome of violet and gray, pulsing in rhythm with Spearfinger's rapid heartbeat. The forest below didn't move with wind but with breath. The trees leaned inward, heavy with silence. Observing.

They all laid in a heap like lovers for a while. Robin and Nick were too happy, and too scared to speak. They never wanted this day to end. This was Shan-gri-la. They came to these woods to fall in love again, and to find bliss. And in this weird way, they succeeded. Paradise was found today, and the couple shared it with their new master.

Robin was the first to move. She rolled over. She lay naked beside Spearfinger in the moss, eyes glazed, a crooked grin frozen across her face. She pushed her perfect ass into Spearfinger's thigh. This was a hint and a question. More please? She never felt so complete, horny, safe, and in love.

Nick moved off and laid on his back, blinking at clouds that didn't exist. His legs trembled. His skin glowed with sweat and something worse—surrender. His large penis lay limp and exposed and to the side. To his surprise, Spearfinger reached out for it, and sweetly fondled it for a while. God, it felt good. "I have never been so happy," he thought.

Spearfinger released the cock, slapped Robin's gorgeous ass, and stood slowly.

Tall. Gleaming. Perfect. Naked.

She looked down at him with something between amusement and pity. She knelt down to him.

"You want to change again, don't you?" she said, running a finger along his chest.

Nick sat up, eyes wide, desperate. He looked over at Robin nervously, then back to his love, "Please."

Spearfinger tilted her head. "You'd give up your body again?"

"Yes."

"Your name?"

"Yes."

"Your mind?"

"Yes! I'll do whatever it takes. I will serve you forever! I LOVE YOU!"

He sat up onto his knees, a familiar position for him now, staring into her eyes with glee.

"I'll be whatever you want."

She smiled. Robin smiled. She was happy for him. For them both.

"No, baby. You'll be *exactly* what you have been this entire time."

She kissed his forehead.

And the ground answered.

The moss trembled.

Then split.

Roots shot up from the soil—wet, black, alive.

They slithered up Nick's legs.

He didn't resist.

They coiled around his waist, his chest, his arms.

They pulled him upright, cruciform.

He gasped.

"Wait... wha-"

The roots wrapped tighter, creaking, groaning, merging with his skin. His toes split into bark. His fingers fused. His ribcage bulged and hardened into rings.

Nick screamed.

His voice echoed once—and then the roots wrapped his throat.

Only his **face** remained. Barely.

And his **cock**—still human.

Still exposed.

Still erect.

Robin giggled.

Drunken. Gleeful.

She stumbled to her feet like a party girl at 2 a.m. and walked up to the rooted Nick, his eyes wide and glassy- as more parts of him disappeared underneath bark, leaves, and twigs.

"Oh my God," she looks over at Spearfinger and then back to what was Nick. She laughed. "He's good wood! That's what you meant!"

Spearfinger cackled.

Robin reached out and tapped his cock gently.

"He's so veiny," she said.

"Still warm," Spearfinger added.

Robin nodded dreamily. "He was a great lay."

"Truly gifted," Spearfinger said. "You mind if I...?"

Spearfinger reached down, rubbed it once.

The tree shivered.

Robin howled laughing.

"Please...," Nick's voice rasped weakly.

"No," Spearfinger said.

They took turns rubbing his large cock. They giggled like school girls. Nick was trying to scream for them to stop, to return him to his normal state, but he just gargled. Barely audible.

Robin bent over, smiled, and enveloped his erect penis with her perfect lips. She deep throated it once. When she ended the tasting, she pop kissed it goodbye.

"Still tasty."

Robin danced around him. "Can I keep him?"

Spearfinger turned to her.

"Do you want my power?"

Robin blinked.

"Yes!" She stood up straight with the posture of a school girl about to receive a gift from a doting uncle and bounced eagerly.

Spearfinger lifted the **mojo** and looped it over Robin's neck.

Robin arched, gasped.

The necklace glowed.

Then went dark.

Robin winced for several seconds, then her eyes opened—black and bottomless.

She took a violent, deep breath in, then released it slowly.

She exhaled into a grin.

Now **Spearfinger** resided in Robin's body. Or maybe Robin is now in the old witch's glorified body. Robin couldn't be sure. But honestly, she doesn't give a fuck. Whatever the case, there is only one sex goddess standing in the clearing, where moments before there were two.

She leaned into the tree.

"Poor Nick. You gave me everything. Your shame. Your cock. Your *root.*"

As the bark slowly covered up Nick's remaining skin, Robin licked his cheek.

He whimpered.

Robin-Spearfinger turned to the woods.

"Let's go hunt," she said out loud to herself.

"I wanted a cheeseburger, but now I think I wanna try a liver," she added, still giggling. "Just once."

"Oh no, we just turned a fresh one into a tree. Whatever shall we do?"

Both voices laughed inside the belly of the statuesque form. Physically speaking, the perfect woman. Completely naked and unashamed and undefeated.

She floated into the air—nude, gorgeous, terrible.

Nick watched, trapped, as his last loves vanished over the trees.

His breath slowed.

His mind dulled.

His cock remained erect.

Over time, he became even less. He forgot memories, words, himself. Even Robin.

***

The forest would often whisper. From time to time in the distance, he could hear two girls giggling. And sometimes, human screams.

Over the years, the tree forgot what giggling was, what girls were and what screams were. He never really snapped out of this mental haze until on these rare occasions: some soft creature would walk over to him, moan friendly tones at his trunk, bend over, and envelope his most sensitive appendage with a moist and firm part of its form. The creature pushed back and forth on this appendage and moaned differently as it did so. The tree also seemed to have a physical reaction to this, and after a few moments, the tree would violently release its own sugars out of its phloem into the friendly creature's warm, tight wetness. After this transaction, the form would moan at it again in soft tones for a while. After more time passed, the form would release its tight grip on the appendage, and it would seem to leave the area after that odd exchange.

This interaction would go on for years. It was obviously the highlight of the tree's existence. But one day, a young boy dared his sister to go kiss the penis-like tree branch sticking out of that weird stump over there. The girl didn't appreciate this game, so she reacted to the bargain by screaming "No!" and with a very large tree branch she found at her feet, she swung it down fast and broke off Nick's dick with one surgical strike. The tree screamed and the traumatized children ran away in terror. Their parents never believed that story.

The End.

Also available:
The Hike – the motion picture
from Big N Funky Productions
and Burning Bulb Publishing